ORGAN VOLUNTARY

ORGAN VOLUNTARY

Tales of a hidden Ireland

Christopher Fitz-Simon

First published 2025 by
THE LILLIPUT PRESS
62–63 Sitric Road,
Arbour Hill,
Dublin 7,
Ireland
www.lilliputpress.ie

10 9 8 7 6 5 4 3 2 1

A CIP record for this title is available from The British Library.

ISBN 978 1 84351 959 1

the arts council
an chomhairle ealaíon
funding literature

Typeset in 11.5 pt on 16 pt Athelas by Susan Waine
Printed in Sweden by ScandBook
Cover Design: Enejda Nasaj

FSC www.fsc.org
MIX
Paper | Supporting responsible forestry
FSC® C021394

BOOKS BY CHRISTOPHER FITZ-SIMON

The Arts in Ireland: A Chronology
The Irish Theatre
The Boys
New Plays from The Abbey Theatre
The Most Beautiful Villages of Ireland
The Abbey Theatre: The First 100 Years
Players and Painted Stage
Eleven Houses: A Memoir of Childhood
Buffoonery and Easy Sentiment
Rise Above!

For Samuel, Ellen, Eva and Emil

CONTENTS

ORGAN VOLUNTARY

Worthy the Lamb! whose dying blood
Now our saints recall to mind;
Rejoice! Rejoice! ...

META MCKELVEY goaded the instrument into a rousing crescendo with subtle movements of her feet, the clattering of her shoes on the wooden pedals drowned by the glorious swell of the Reverend Sabine Baring Gould's triumphant hymn. She was able to see round the corner of the organ case that Mr Flegg was almost apoplectic in his efforts to pump sufficient air into the bellows to keep the music going; it occurred to her that he should soon join his sister in retirement and pass the task to some younger person, one of those hefty fellows from the Student Christian Movement perhaps, for it would be a terrible slur on the parish should he collapse from a heart attack because of over-devotion to his Sunday duties. On retiring, he could certainly rejoice in a job well done.

Easter was the proper time for rejoicing, Miss McKelvey believed. Especially this Easter, when she would definitely feel disposed to rejoice – though in a rather private way which she could hardly have anticipated the previous year.

Miss McKelvey, whose day-job was Senior Assistant in

the District Library, had presided at the organ in St Phelim's on Sundays and Saints' Days for almost thirty years, on an annual stipend of what had been £150 and was now €162. The figure in Euro made it look larger, but this was immaterial. Playing the organ was a voluntary activity and she was serving the parish – and, she was not shy to observe, serving her God – by making her talents available in the most suitable way. She would have played for nothing, indeed, had she been asked. But she had not been asked; nor had she been offered an additional honorarium when the parish, and consequently the duties of its voluntary workers, had expanded. That, however, had been some years before the appointment of the Rev. Victor Corscadden.

St Phelim's parish had indeed increased in population following half a century's decline when it seemed that only their Romanist neighbours were enjoying greater numbers. A modern chapel-of-ease dedicated to Pope Paul VI had been erected near the council estate – its presence causing some anxiety among several of Miss McKelvey's acquaintance – built almost entirely of violet glass and surrounded by an all too symbolically extensive car-park. However, Canon Hazleton, the rector of St Phelim's, had attended the dedication ceremony in a spirit of goodwill and this had been noted in both communities as an action that could neither be gainsaid nor forgotten. Since then the synthetic fabrics company had established itself on the outskirts of the town, causing an influx of higher-paid executives, and this was followed by a development of some two-dozen rather fine suburban homes on the Monaghan road, causing the community to grow once again and occasioning the appointment of a curate dedicated specifically to St Phelim's, up to then the ageing Canon having to divide his responsibilities between St Phelim's and the rural churches at Athlurcan and Beulah's Mills.

The arrival of the Reverend Victor Corscadden brought a new sense of zest and purpose to the parish. He was twenty-six, very fair, with blue eyes and white lashes. His landlady, Mrs Moodie, described her temporary lodger as being 'of cherubic countenance'; while Mrs Walmsley, the doctor's wife, remarked that he might more properly be described as 'Albino'. Yet, in spite of his slightly ungainly form, Mr Corscadden proved himself to be unusually energetic, and it seemed that in the unexpectedly expansionist mood of the 1980s he should disclose qualities that surely benefited his new flock. His previous incumbency – yet it was not exactly an incumbency, more an administrative position – had been with the Dublin University Mission to Belfast where he had started a debating society and a drama class; and he had doubled the membership of the basketball club. His knowledge of organisational procedures had enabled him to uncover several unsuspected sources of revenue from the European Social Fund.

As soon as Mr Corscadden arrived in Clementstown, he formed a committee to oversee the renovation of church property. During his first week he identified dry rot in the apse, and he annoyed Miss McKelvey by suggesting that, due to a perforated rain gutter, water had almost certainly seeped into the organ pipes which was why they gave that occasional splutter. He proposed that the rambling eighteenth-century Rectory – vacant since Canon Hazleton had moved into more manageable 'chambers' in the town – should be restored and placed on the open market. A bungalow, better suited to the needs of the present-day clerical household, should be built between the pleasant grove of umbrella pines and the attractive Victorian lych-gate which, in turn, should be repaired to serve as the entrance to this new Rectory. The sale brochure should point out that the historic building was notable as the birthplace of the maternal grandfather of Governor Bowen of Queensland and had once been visited by Charlotte Brontë.

The members of the committee were asked to distribute a leaflet – which Mr Corscadden devised – to any of their acquaintance who had Clementstown connections at home or abroad, soliciting donations for the renovation of the church, which he described as a unique example of the Church of Ireland's ancient heritage, the site having been connected with Christian worship as far back as the time of the Saint in whose memory it was named.

In the meantime Mr Corscadden lived comfortably enough in Moodie's Lough View Guest House. Mrs Moodie, the widow of a local second-hand furniture dealer and a noted gardener, reported to Miss McKelvey that their curate was wont to receive telephone calls from a young lady, and it was thus assumed in the parish that the need for the new bungalow by the lych-gate would in due course be explained when their pastor took it upon himself to announce his engagement. Indeed, a source close to his previous employment revealed that there was certainly a woman in the offing, and that she was a dedicated social-worker in Sligo.

To the intense surprise of the committee – almost all the

members of which were dubious about the curate's expansionist plans but felt that he had been too short a time with them for their misgivings to be boldly expressed – money, in modest though not inconsiderable sums, started to come in for the restoration project. Some very successful beetle-drives were arranged by an elderly lady with – they felt – more time on her hands than sense, but participants were inclined to donate their entire winnings at the end of each evening. A recently arrived director of the synthetic fabrics factory, who had been well known in the amateur drama world, organised a splendid production of *Annie, Get Your Gun!* cast entirely from local talent, drawing crowds to the Coliseum Cinema for a full week. The Roman Catholic parish donated a handsome percentage – it was not stated exactly what percentage – of the proceeds from that year's Lily of Clementstown contest, no doubt in acknowledgement of the good relationship created earlier by Canon Hazleton. All this was a start. Then an industrialist in Ontario sent a donation of $50,000 in memory of his parents who had emigrated from Clementstown in the 1960s with little more than the clothes they stood up in, his only stipulation being that a plaque in their memory be erected in a prominent position in the nave.

Mr Corscadden's face grew rounder and chubbier as his plans prospered. Inspired by his success, he introduced several liturgical innovations into the Order of Worship. All these occasioned additional hours for Miss McKelvey who, up to the present time, had to play only for matins and evensong on Sundays and a very few Holy Days – apart from weddings and funerals, for which she usually received a pleasing gift-voucher from the families involved. Mr Corscadden instituted a Sung Eucharist on Second Sundays and it became his way to announce special services, at very short notice, to mark what Miss McKelvey, in her heart of hearts, felt were rather minor fixtures in the church calendar, such as Septuagesima, Rogation Days and the Circumcision of St Chrysostom of Antioch.

Mr Corscadden also caused some unspoken concern by his decision to broaden the scope of exhibition at the Harvest Thanksgiving. 'Sheaves of corn and vegetable marrows are very right and proper as examples of the Lord's bounty,' he told a meeting of the Mothers' Union, 'but is it not the case that we of this parish subsist on the results of our industry in fields that include more than mere farming and horticulture?' Thus, bales of synthetic fabrics and polystyrene containers of electrical goods made their appearance in the chancel on that particular Sunday, and Mrs Walmsley's famous button dahlias and Mrs Moodie's mauve Michaelmas daisies were relegated to the south transept. Some sense of disquiet must have reached the curate because the following year he requested a more meaningful return to the neighbourhood's farms and fields. Miss McKelvey was invited to select an anthem with a pastoral theme – but the manufactured goods retained their place.

It was not unnatural that Miss McKelvey should feel that her honorarium – though she fully recognised it was only an honorarium – should be increased. She knew that it was not customary in such matters to make a direct approach, so she enlisted the advice of Mrs Walmsley as to how she might discreetly proceed. Mrs Walmsley, who always preferred to call a spade a spade, was of the opinion that she should write directly to the curate, listing her hours and stating that her duties now almost amounted to that of a professional organist in a city parish. She advised that Miss McKelvey should make her case very clearly, though she need not name an actual figure. Miss McKelvey wondered if she should enlist Canon Hazelton as a go-between but Mrs Walmsley said definitely not: that would only spread the load and anyway the Canon was said to be on the point of retiring into a home, owing to poor health, which really meant dotage.

Miss McKelvey, weighing the pros and cons as she went about her work in the library, decided that she could not bring herself to express herself so crudely. She feared that the Reverend Corscadden would reply that she was surely not dependent upon her earnings as organist of St Phelim's, which was of course true. She was afraid he might think she was of a mercenary disposition, when she was anything but. All she required was some small appreciation of her talent as a musician. She therefore did nothing, pursing her lips over the keyboard when she heard a special evening of meditation announced that required a sympathetic musical background. At one such event she deliberately chose swell-to-great on the stops before playing a loud chromatic cadence expressive of irritation as Mr Corscadden ascended the pulpit so that he had to wait for its echoes to die away before commencing his address. Mr Flegg inclined his head in an understanding manner in the gloom of the organ loft – a wink would have been out of place – while exerting himself at the bellows in support of her tasteful protest.

On the morning of the Fifth Sunday in Lent, while entering the church grounds in advance of the congregation to prepare her music, Miss McKelvey observed Mrs Moodie, wearing her overcoat and hat, waving from the door of the guest house. She waited as Mrs Moodie crossed the road.

'Good morning, Betty. You're out early.'

'The same as yourself, Meta. I hope you haven't many of those down-in-the-mouth hymns for us today.'

'Lent's a solemn time', said Miss McKelvey. 'You can't just pick the joyful ones. Any news?'

'She's here,' replied Mrs Moodie, giving a twitch of her shoulder in the direction of her house.

'Who's that?'

'The fiancée. She arrived last night. In her own car too – a Ford Fiesta.'

'And himself?' Miss McKelvey had no need to articulate her query more expansively.

'He booked a room for her yesterday at tea-time only, said he'd just had a phone-call to say she was coming. Sure enough, I took the call and handed it to him but I was too busy making a Madeira cake to bother with who it might be. I gave her a soda farl and a cup of tea when she arrived about nine o'clock. A wee dark one in a blue costume.'

'We'll see her in church then,' said Miss McKelvey, anticipating the scene.

'He took a farl too, to keep her company. I left them sitting in the front room.'

From her perch in the gallery, Miss McKelvey could observe the neat young woman in the blue coat and skirt sitting in the front pew on the left that was reserved for the clergyman and his kindred. It would be obvious to the whole congregation who she was. Mr Corscadden should have asked Mr Flegg to show her to one of the visitors' pews, for she was not Mrs Corscadden yet.

Before starting his sermon, the curate announced that the Easter service this year would, in a tangible fashion, emphasise the renewal of life. Parishioners were cordially invited to decorate the church with daffodils and bluebells. They were also invited to introduce living things. He envisaged a clutch of chickens, perhaps, and said he would be glad to receive similar suggestions, especially anything that would make the ceremony more significant for the children.

As Miss McKelvey was leaving by the vestry door, Mr Corscadden introduced her to the young woman in blue as 'my friend Maureen Stokes'. Miss McKelvey said she was delighted to meet her, and would she be staying long? Miss Stokes said only till that evening but she hoped to be back at Easter. While the curate was locking up the communion vessels, the two ladies strolled down the gravel path, the younger admiring the view and the beauty of the building. Miss McKelvey took the opportunity of agreeing that it was indeed a very handsome church – everyone thought so – and that Mr Corscadden seemed to be bringing new life to it. She also remarked – with a little laugh, as if the thought had just come to her – that she didn't know how she was going to manage with all the extra services they seemed to be having nowadays. 'Indeed,' she continued, 'we nearly need two organists here!' At this point they were joined by Mr Corscadden, and Miss McKelvey was left wondering if her message had sunk in, and if it would be repeated as significant over the boiled mutton and semolina pudding in Mrs Moodie's guest house.

Preparations for the Easter Celebration proceeded apace. It was understood that the Bishop would attend, to inaugurate the Restoration Plan. A niece of Mrs Walmsley was invited to bring her pet rabbit, its hutch to be placed on view in the porch. It was hoped that this rabbit, a doe, would by that time have produced a litter: no one arriving at the church, Mr Corscadden was certain, would fail to comprehend what it was saying. Mr Mawhinney, a farmer and a well-respected church-warden, was persuaded to bring a lamb, which would be carried in procession by the children and then tethered to the altar-rail with a pretty garland of flowers round its neck. Mr Mawhinney had expressed some doubt about the likely behaviour of the lamb, separated from its mother, but Mr Corscadden cast all reservations aside by declaring that its tiny bleat would hardly be an interruption; in fact, it would draw the attention of the young people to the Miracle of Spring.

Miss McKelvey was asked to find a hymn in which lambs featured. She leafed through the hymnal and found, Worthy the Lamb, whose dying blood Now our saints recall to mind; she then consulted the index in *Anthems Selected for Small Choirs* and chose 'O Crucified Redeemer by Stainer' because it was short and would not take much time to practise. The parts were simple enough too, and if Captain Coote-Conyngham found the bass line beyond him he could sing the top line an octave lower and this would not be noticed since the Eakins brothers could both read the dots and their contribution would cover the Captain's inadequacy – after all, a choir was a unified thing and not a collection of individuals. After the practice, she was surprised to find herself congratulated by Mr Corscadden, whom she could not have seen seated below her in the nave. He told her that her Herculean efforts had not gone unnoticed, so she assumed that the remark she had made to Miss Stokes must have been passed on.

'It does take up a great deal of my time,' she said. 'Indeed, I'm not sure that I'll be able to continue next year because I'll be working in the branch library at Beulah's Mills and that's a fair distance – with the price of petrol and all.'

'I'm sure you'll find a way of overcoming that,' said Mr Corscadden. 'I believe there's a new bus service, for instance.'

'It isn't the money,' continued Miss McKelvey boldly; 'it isn't the money at all. Though indeed,' she added quickly, realising that of course it was the money, 'as I always say, "the labourer is worthy of his hire".'

'Of course! Of course! An apt quotation from the Gospel according to St Luke, if I'm not mistaken.' His pale blue eyes searched hers and then flickered away in the direction of a tall marble monument erected in memory of those who had died in the Ashanti War which Mr Flegg was dusting with a bunch of turkey feathers tied to the end of a bamboo cane. 'I'll see about that.'

Miss McKelvey returned home, wondering if he would. An increase of one hundred and sixty-two Euro would be about right. He could hardly offer less, in these days of rising costs and spiralling inflation. Yes, she would certainly accept €162. She was relieved that the matter had been so easily aired. She felt a lightness in herself, an enthusiasm for the work in hand which she had not experienced since she had arrived in Clementstown as a trainee librarian all those years ago and Mr Hazleton had discovered her talent for music. Indeed, the anniversary of her arrival would be Easter and surely this would be the appropriate time for her talent and dedication to be fully recognised.

On Easter Sunday Miss McKelvey attended early Communion. Although her presence as organist was not required she decided she would play a suitable voluntary – a voluntary voluntary! – making sure of course that Mr Flegg would be on hand to pump the bellows. Then she would go home to breakfast, returning for the important service at eleven o'clock. She was surprised to see a large sheep grazing among the tombstones and then Mr Mawhinney appeared from behind a crumbling mausoleum shooing a lamb in the direction of the sheep which proved, by the antiphonal bleating that ensued, to be its mother.

'I brought her along so the lamb wouldn't fret,' said the kindly Mr Mawhinney. 'If the two of them are here for a couple of hours, they'll get used to the place. Then we can take the lamb into the church for the service – it'll be better that way.'

Seeing that the ewe and the lamb were perfectly content in the unfamiliar surroundings – the ewe discovering undreamt of delights in the lush grass surrounding the graves, the lamb deriving sustenance from the ewe – Mr Mawhinney backed his tractor and trailer into the road and made for home and a good Ulster fry.

On entering the porch, Miss McKelvey was charmed by the scent of narcissi: Mrs Walmsley and her helpers had done themselves proud. There was no sign of the rabbit but she assumed it would make its appearance at the right time. There were only a dozen people at Communion, most of them elderly, though she noticed that Miss Stokes was present. Miss McKelvey played a solemn Canzonetta by Buxtehude and, when the short service was over, she arranged the music books for the members of her choir in readiness for eleven o'clock. She descended from the gallery to find the curate standing at the foot of the stairs.

'Ah, Miss McKelvey, what an appropriate tune! You always pick the right thing.'

'It's a nice piece, right enough,' Miss McKelvey agreed.

'About that other matter. I thought we should have a little word.'

'Oh yes?'

'I've been thinking it over.'

'You promised you would.'

'I've thought it over very deeply, I may say. I've also been talking to the Bishop.'

Miss McKelvey was surprised and elated. She had not imagined that the Bishop, that pleasant Dr Goode with the Cork accent, would have been consulted about her stipend.

'Yes, I've spoken to the Bishop. Not on your particular matter' – Miss McKelvey looked slightly disappointed – 'but on more general matters regarding parish economics. The Bishop takes the view that because of the very high expenses involved in our restoration scheme, we should all, ehm, tighten our belts, so to speak. True, we've been very successful so far but there's still a shortfall of nearly thirty thousand euro. I think you'll agree that in the interests of the parish we should defer – that is – and I hope you'll understand – we should not increase our expenses, such as the honoraria we pay to our voluntary helpers, for quite some time.' He paused, as if waiting for a response. 'Till we see how things are going.'

Miss McKelvey was so disconcerted she could not think of anything to say. The curate continued, 'We must all bear the burden for the general good.'

Not quite sure if she had understood correctly, Miss McKelvey felt a little faint. She could hardly argue her point, let alone make a scene, in the church – especially since she could see Miss Stokes waiting by the vestry door.

'Do I understand – ?'

'I'm afraid so. I am – the Bishop and I are – unable to increase your honorarium.'

All Miss McKelvey could say was 'Thank you!' as she turned and walked down the centre aisle and out into the churchyard, at the same time wondering what she was thanking him for. At least she had preserved her dignity in front of that rabbit-faced – yes, he looked just like a big white rabbit, all he lacked was the pink eyes! And that little scheming hussy from Sligo – she probably had put him up to it. Such a thing would never have happened in Canon Hazleton's time, though she had never approached him on such a topic: there had been no need.

She hadn't the heart to poach the egg she had promised herself. All she took for breakfast was a cup of tea and a sprinkling of All-bran in a bowl. She did not hasten back to the church, arriving calmly at five minutes to eleven when she found a group of girls tittering in the porch at the sight of the large Angora rabbit which was observing them from the confines of its wooden hutch, its nose twitching incessantly – a tic she thought was probably shared by the curate: she would watch him to see if this was the case, and probably it was. As she made her way to the gallery stairs, she passed Mr Flegg, who was helping a young woman arrange a large wicker basket out of which stretched the slender neck of a goose. The plaintive remonstrations of the disorientated goslings issued from beneath.

'Quare goings on,' remarked Mr Flegg sotto voce as she passed.

Miss McKelvey selected her stops for the processional hymn, 'The Strife is o'er, the Battle done!' while Mr Flegg pumped the bellows. She was now quite sure he'd collapse sooner rather than later and Mr Corscadden would have to install an electric organ: that would cost him a pretty penny! The group from the girls' school processed up the centre aisle bearing posies, the older members of the congregation smiling sentimentally at this traditional image of childhood. Then the boys filed in, smirking at the attention they were receiving, carrying baskets of eggs which they set down in front of the lectern. Miss McKelvey could just see the beaming countenance of Mr Corscadden, nodding in benign anticipation to the Bishop as they awaited their entrance. The Bishop inclined his head in appreciation and followed the procession, taking up his position within the sanctuary and handing his crook to the curate who leaned it carefully against the carved reredos. Miss McKelvey allowed herself the thought that this was all a bit Romish; next thing they'd be crossing themselves and wafting incense around the place. The hymn came to an end. She played a very loud 'Amen!' and was startled – as indeed was everyone else – by a fearsome screech, which could only have been made by the goose, demonstrating her displeasure at the volume of the music.

Mr Corscadden led the prayers, his face displaying a gentle tolerance at this avine indiscretion. The anthem passed off tolerably well, Miss McKelvey deciding on a rather slower tempo than the one indicated in the book since the work was new to the choir. She was pleased to hear Captain Coote-Conyngham singing some of the right notes – she brought out the bass part to give him confidence. During the Bishop's address, which was on the subject of Giving – '

'Do unto others as you would have them do unto you', a text which Miss McKelvey thought somewhat inappropriate – a distant bleating was heard from the churchyard as Mr Mawhinney captured the lamb in readiness for the offertory procession. The sidesmen took up the collection while Mr Mawhinney held the lamb gently in his arms before handing it to the little girl in the floral pinafore whose assignment it was to carry it to the altar. She was to present it to the curate who would then speak a little homily of his own devising.

The collection plates were received. The lamb struggled, baa-ing loudly, but the little girl held onto it bravely. Mr Corscadden accepted the frightened animal from the girl, who retreated, blushing. In order to give point to the ritual, Miss McKelvey played some decorative chords, strepito, whereupon the goose added her voice to that of the lamb. No sooner had she done so than a much louder and more purposeful bleating was heard, and the sheep, her mother's heart rent by the crying of her child, rushed in through the open porch and up the aisle, knocking over the little girl and causing some elder parishioners to clutch their pitch-pine book-rests in alarm.

Miss McKelvey, who had been instructed to keep playing until it appeared that Mr Corscadden was ready to speak, found herself performing a series of arpeggios and trills, rather than the more sedate improvisation which she'd had in mind. The ewe, failing to perceive the lamb in the clergyman's arms, ran down the side aisle pursued by Mr Mawhinney who, on turning the corner by the war-memorial, knocked over the goose's basket. A catch opened and out flew the goose, intent (like the sheep) on protecting her young. The goslings were quite safe under the upturned creel, but their disorientated and angry mother could not see them, flying at the nearest apparent child-molester who happened to be the unfortunate Mr Mawhinney, who had managed to corral his sheep behind the font and was attempting to pull it in the direction of the porch by grasping handfuls of its wool. The goose, flapping her wings, bit savagely at his legs. Instead of restoring her to the goslings, he unwisely snatched a copy of the *Church of Ireland Gazette* which he flapped at the flapping goose, hissing 'Get back! Get back!' Miss McKelvey accompanied these proceedings on the organ.

The little girl's family bustled around her. Her knee was only slightly grazed but the psychological hurt was much greater and she was weeping uncontrollably. Mr Corscadden, feeling he should offer solicitation, handed the lamb to a gentleman in the front pew but not before stepping into a punnet of duck eggs. The Bishop, sensible and experienced man that he was, remained within the sanctuary in a meditative posture.

Miss McKelvey, realising that these unrehearsed additions to the service might continue for some time, selected the Ebnezer Prout fugue from the heap of music by her elbow, performing it with much feeling as duty clearly directed. The fugue seemed to infuriate the goose even further until a sensible sidesman released the goslings and shooed them – their mother in close attendance – out into the churchyard. Mr Mawhinney gave the sheep a sharp slap on the snout with the rolled-up Gazette and it followed the hissing and squeaking birds.

The parishioner in the front row, sensing a trickle of something on his trouser-leg, flung the unfortunate lamb into the aisle. It made its way towards the darkness of the vestry door, into which it disappeared. Mr Flegg, who had resolutely maintained his task of pumping the organ, feeling that his duties as verger must now take priority, left the organ loft. The notes of the fugue died away like the last gasps of an early martyr. Mr Flegg descended the stairs and followed the lamb into the vestry, closing the door, the better to effect its capture. There was now silence in the church – an awkward silence, Miss McKelvey realised, for without Mr Flegg they would have to sing the final hymn, 'Worthy the Lamb', unaccompanied. She saw Mr Corscadden retracing his steps in the direction of the altar. He appeared to step on something that had not been there before, which caused him to slip and measure his considerable girth on the Stoke tiles, cracking his head on the chancel steps.

After this, there was nothing for it but that the Bishop should step forward and pronounce the Blessing. Miss McKelvey felt disposed to play Handel's 'Hallelujah Chorus' – and indeed she would have done so had there been someone to pump the bellows.

When the Reverend Victor Corscadden was discharged from Cavan General Hospital four months later, he found that the fund-raising scheme was progressing quite satisfactorily under the direction of Captain Coote-Conyngham. The Georgian rectory had been sold for what everyone considered to be a very satisfactory sum to a celebrated dress-designer who intended to hold the launch of her seasonal collections in its oval drawing-room. The locum curate – on the advice of Bishop Goode, it appeared – had greatly reduced the number of special services. The organist, Miss McKelvey, passed some remark which, in his somewhat dazed state, Mr Corscadden did not fully comprehend, concerning labourers and their hire. Meanwhile, the Select Vestry had come to the fairly obvious conclusion that they would save a great deal of money by not building a new rectory and so an apartment was purchased for the incumbent in a new block facing the cemetery.

The matter of the Easter service was never mentioned. Miss McKelvey and Mr Flegg felt it would be disrespectful to the church to allude to it. On the following Sunday Mr Flegg and his sister invited Miss McKelvey to luncheon, and she had wondered if they wished to advert to the topic in order to exorcise the whole fearful episode from their minds; but she was glad when she found that it was a purely social occasion because a female cousin of theirs from Dublin was present and they certainly wouldn't have touched on a topic that might have brought the local parish into disrepute. Miss Flegg provided a rather lumpy brown Windsor soup and an over-sweet cherry trifle but the roast lamb was delicious – exceptionally tender and succulent – and Miss McKelvey wondered if it was the effect of the unaccustomed glass of sherry which she had taken before the meal or if she really did see Mr Flegg wink at her while carving it.

A SNOWMAN IN JULY

'He's basically selfish, is our Tom, I'm afraid,' declared Angela MacNaughten, B.A., Dip. Ed., dunking her goldgrain biscuit into her cup of Nescafé, and then adding, 'He never even goes on a holiday abroad.'

'As if that had anything to do with it,' Dr Rainey remarked, giving a surreptitious raise of an eyebrow in the direction of Mervyn Bleakley, M.A., Dip. Ed., who deftly transformed an incipient titter into a cough.

They were taking their mid-morning break in the staff common room of Eglantine College at a moment when their colleague, Thomas Griffin, M.A., Dip. Ed., was absent on library duty.

'But look at it this way,' Dr Rainey pursued. 'If he were considering a holiday abroad, who would go with him? Would you fancy a fling on the Côte-de-Whatnot with him yourself?'

'Catch me!' replied Angela with unreserved emphasis. 'But do you really think I'd be invited?' she continued, sensing that she was being sent up.

'Oh, I just wondered if the absence of an invitation was occasioned by a mild – how shall I put it? – a mild dose of la grappe amer?'

Well used to the Doctor's ribbing, Angela continued: 'Joking apart, Walter, shouldn't a man do something with his money? I mean who's going to benefit from it if he doesn't make use of it himself?'

'How do you know he hasn't a secret mistress out in Helen's Bay whom he visits every Saturday after hockey?' Mervyn enquired with a comparatively straight face.

'Huh! Some mistress that'd be!' Angela replied with a fair attempt at what she considered to be a hollow laugh. She sucked at the remains of her biscuit and rose to pick up a pile of exercise books from the lid of the piano. Then, as she was leaving the room to return to her class: 'People who don't share their lives with others are basically selfish, that's what I say. He's interested in no one but himself, if you ask me.'

'I wouldn't dare to ask her,' Dr Rainey said when she had closed the door, leaving a pleasant whiff of muguet des bois behind her to mingle with the aroma of burnt toast. 'Can it be that she has experienced a rebuff – a very civil rebuff of course – from our chum?'

Mervyn mused to himself on the subject of Angela's life, wondering if she shared it with others and, if not, how she viewed herself in the scheme of things.

'Lookat,' said Dr Rainey, bringing him back down to realities, 'can you picture the two of them together in a pension at Beaulieu-sur-Mer? Ooh là là!'

Tom Griffin was now in his forty-sixth year, having passed that significant birthday five years back without declaring it to others. He entertained mild apprehensions about becoming a fogey, and seriously hoped that he wasn't showing fogeyish traits, as so many of his profession seemed to do at too early an age, eccentric traits accepted as 'amusing' by colleagues and pupils alike. Such peculiarities, he felt, were due to the repetition syndrome – repetition each year as prescribed texts were studied once again, occasioning the same old jokes and creating the same polite laughter. There were also repeated actions, designed to entertain and therefore gain the compliance of unruly boys – such as that of his friend Pedlow who, when there was too much chatter in his classroom, would take a pin from his lapel and cast it on the floor with the words, 'No, I can't hear it drop'. This had gained him the nickname 'Pinny Pedlow'. Nicknames often gave the wrong impression, with their play on words, as if Pedlow wore a pinafore.

The thing was, of course, to keep a rein on oneself, to observe one's conduct constantly and critically. Tom faced the next decade with equanimity, a kind of passive defiance as if daring himself to prove that he was not slipping inexorably into middle age – for he was doing no such thing! His physical appearance belied his years. He was neither obese nor scrawny. He could name several colleagues of roughly the same age whose complexions – and stomachs – proclaimed an excessive indoor existence circumscribed by the classroom, the suburban living-room and the pub. His hair showed no signs of recession, though these days a shiny pate was taken as a mark of masculinity rather than the opposite. He took exercise by refereeing the middle-school hockey practice twice a week, by always walking to and from the school, a distance of almost two miles, and by fairly regular hikes in the Mourne mountains on routes recommended by the Naturalists' Field Club.

Such matters as appearance and health, however, did not often intrude upon his mind: they were taken as a given. He was much prouder of the fact that, in spite of all his twenty years in the service of the same school, he had not become institutionalised. He had never been lampooned in the school magazine under a too easily identified nom de guerre as a crank of one kind or another. He did not think it remotely possible that he would ever become a Mr Chips, even if he stayed on until the official retiring age. In other words, he saw himself as a very normal person, outwardly and inwardly, in a profession which – as he only had to confirm by observing certain other members of the staff – gave asylum to a uniquely high percentage of crackpots.

Mr Griffin regarded some of his colleagues with mild disapprobation, attributing their eccentricities to the fact that they boarded on the premises not only during terms but in the holidays as well, failing to enjoy the normal social life that he did, such as attendance at concerts in the Waterfront Hall or the foreign screen series in the Film Theatre. Dr Rainey, the Head of the Science Department, was known to spend much of his leisure hours in the Physics Lab, so that he was becoming – or perhaps had become – the prototype alchemist, muttering over stews and potions. There was also the case of Miss Angela MacNaughten, an experienced History teacher, who, according to widespread rumour originating with young men who had long passed out of the school into the wider world, was said to have sat at her high desk in a posture from which the young fellows in the front row could without difficulty discern an absence of essential underclothing. Possibly this had happened only once, and probably it was quite accidental, but it became an established myth of the kind that, with retelling, progresses to regular fact. When it came to the ears of the Headmaster, he was at his wit's end as to how to convey his concern to the much-respected teacher; eventually he lost his nerve and installed a new design of desk supported by a useful set of drawers in which to keep such items as blackboard dusters and boxes of chalks, that concealed all but the head and shoulders of the incumbent. (The term drawers caused considerable merriment in the Lower Fifth throughout one endless Michaelmas term: Miss MacNaughten has wooden drawers.)

Tom Griffin did not live in school but in a flat. He had the upper floor of a two-storey Edwardian house on Colenso Parade rented from the Robinsons, the elderly couple who lived downstairs. It had a really marvellous view across the Botanic Gardens and the river towards the hills of County Down. Mrs Robinson took an 'interest' in him, and although he did his own catering, she would 'run over' the apartment with her vacuum cleaner once a week and would also empty the contents of his laundry basket into her washing-machine so that when he returned from school on Tuesdays he would find his shirts beautifully ironed and laid out on his bed. Mrs Robinson was forever making coy little remarks about her tenant's single state, implying that she fully expected to be deprived of these domestic arrangements when Miss Right made her appearance on the scene.

Tom took these sallies with customary good humour.

Sometimes, indeed, the picture of such a person floated into his mind; he could see her seated in an armchair beside a glowing coal fire doing something with her hands; darning socks, perhaps. Other times the image merged into something more up-to-date, such as this person returning from work – in the Civil Service, it might be, having shopped at the supermarket on the way home – announcing that she had booked seats for the Opera House on the spur of the moment and they'd snatch an early dinner. He could not have been aware that his colleagues in the common-room sometimes speculated as to why he had not married; but, if he had been, it would not have caused him the slightest discomposure.

'Hello, sir! Day-dreaming, sir?'

'What?' Mr Griffin, reflectively strolling under the plane trees in the direction of the University Bookshop, turned his head abruptly to find a young man on a bicycle freewheeling alongside him. 'Oh hello, McLean.'

'Davey, sir. The formalities of Eglantine may now be cast aside.'

'Of course. Well, hello, Davey, how's the world treating you?'

'Ruthlessly, sir. The varsity is the pits. I'm thinking of joining the Territorials.'

'A moment of disillusion within the groves of academe?'

'A moment of shaggin' frustration, if you'll pardon the colloquialism. Occasioned by Provençal and Catalan – dead languages.'

'Ah, now,' said Mr Griffin in mock defence of his two pet subjects, 'they do have interesting literatures.'

'They have very boring literatures. Critics, who are really

only interested in linguistics, cracking up rather dim stories as if they were something better than tales for wee childer.'

'Do I divine correctly that you've failed an exam?'

'Actually I got a First!'

A very brilliant student, thought Mr Griffin of his former pupil, as he listened to Davey McLean's description of his first year at Queen's University, Davey propelling his bicycle by kicking the kerb as they moved along together. He was saying that when the summer term was over he was going to work in a bakery owned by a distant relative in order to earn money to supplement his accommodation costs next year, his grant being barely enough to cover tuition. Several of his friends had spent their spare cash the previous summer on fares to European countries in search of jobs that hadn't materialised and so had had to undertake menial work in the city throughout the following year in order to stay alive, allowing little or no time for socialising. He didn't mind working in the bakery during the vacation and the very early start in the morning meant free afternoons and evenings.

Outside the bookshop Mr Griffin listened attentively, admiring the youngster's resource.

'Well, so long, sir. Thanks for the chat.'

Mr Griffin, whose contribution to the chat had been monosyllabic, nodded its termination.

'I might call you sometime, sir, if you wouldn't mind, about the 'Cantilène de Saint Eulalie'. It has me round the twist.'

'You'll find me in the phone book. And I'm usually to be found in person in Kelly's on the corner of Comber Street on Friday evenings, around nine. I'm not over-enthusiastic about pub life, as you may guess, but I do like to keep in touch with the Real People, if that doesn't sound too pretentious.'

'It does sound disgustingly pretentious,' said Davey with an exaggerated grimace. 'You can count me as one of the Real People, with my rustic background. Salût!'

Mr Griffin browsed in the bookshop for twenty minutes, emerging with a new paperback edition of *Chants Languedocois du Moyen Age* which contained drawings of churches and castles in the region, many of them recently restored. It half crossed his mind that it would be interesting to see them as they were background to his special area of literary study.

He was quite surprised the following Friday when the door of the almost empty pub opened and Davey McLean came in. He looked round in a hesitant kind of way, as if unsure if he'd come to the right place, or apprehensive of not being welcome in some group or other – the look of a person unused to the niceties of pub behaviour. It took Mr Griffin several seconds to realise that Davey was looking for him, so he waved energetically from the shadowy corner in which he was seated, out of range of the television screen that was silently presenting a football match in some other country. Davey approached, picking his way among the low tables and stools.

'You said I might find you here.'

'Of course, of course – do join me!' Mr Griffin found himself suddenly hearty. He gestured effusively, indicating a place on the moquette seat beside him, moving his khaki anorak out of the way. 'What are you having?'

'You're sure I'm not intruding?'

'Not in the slightest. The man with whom I was having an animated discussion about our chances in Saturday's match has just left because he needed to see a game on another channel. Sit down and let me get you a drink.'

'Thanks. A beer.'

Mr Griffin signalled the barman, holding up his bottle and miming 'Two'. Their conversation was formal at first. They talked about the tyranny of exams, about the growing problems of unemployment, about the book that Mr Griffin had been leafing through until he was joined by the football enthusiast. He let Davey buy a second round, afraid he might appear patronising if he treated him again. Later their talk took on less of the restraint that is common between those whose former relationship has been that of teacher and pupil. It emerged that Davey was from a small country town where his mother and her sister ran a newsagents' shop, his father having died suddenly while Davey was still at primary school. He said he'd won a scholarship to Eglantine College, inaugurated by a former pupil.

'Oh yes,' said Mr Griffin, 'that would be the Irvine Bursary – it was set up by a man who did well in shipping and was intended, as far as I can recall, "for the scholastically promising sons of impoverished families in the County of Fermanagh" – would that be it?'

'Dead on,' said Davey, 'though I wouldn't have described us as exactly impoverished. Our business was doing OK though not so OK that I could have afforded to go to boarding school.'

Mr Griffin drained his glass. 'It's a pleasant place, Fermanagh.'

'You've obviously never been there.'

'I've passed through it many times – going to Donegal.'

'That's all it's fit for: passing through. Ulster's alimentary canal.'

'Well then,' Mr Griffin was deliberately facetious, 'aren't you the lucky man to have been given the opportunity of tasting the delights of Ulster's metropolis?'

There was a pause. Davey's voice took on a serious note. 'Yes, I'm very lucky. More than I can say.'

The conversation turned to the topic for which Davey said he'd come to discuss – 'these damned early French poets. Like a tutorial, if you can bear that.'

For Mr Griffin it was the simplest thing in the world to repeat what he had always retained in his head since, when at university himself, he had been awarded the Helen Waddell Memorial Prize for an essay on The Troubadours. True, there had been only one other entry in the competition, but his had been judged as by far the more comprehensive and he'd put that down to the fact that the subject was a genuine enthusiasm. He dilated on the origins of the chansons de geste at some length. 'Is all this very boring?' he asked after about half an hour. Davey said it definitely was not and Mr Griffin insisted on buying another round. Davey, laughing, said, 'Alright, I couldn't have got it anyway because I only have twenty p left!'

Davey's face was pink, Mr Griffin observed, whether from admission of his financial embarrassment or from taking more drink than he was used to it was impossible to say. He was quite a slight young man. He had a fringe of what one might take for black hair, except that the light from the imitation Tudor lantern above his head brought out a faint iridescence of copper. His face was square and might have run to pudginess were it not for the possibility that he did not get enough to eat. His eyes, which had a deliberate look, suggesting a straightforward attitude to life, were a very dark grey.

Mr Griffin found himself talking about his own life to an extent that was unusual for him. He talked of the school and how teaching in such a place might seem, to the disaffected spectator, little more than an academic treadmill; but how very satisfying he found it in spite of minor irritations of a purely administrative nature.

'We appreciated what you did for us,' said Davey.

'What?'

'You were very well liked.'

Mr Griffin was surprised. 'I don't look for adulation.'

'That's the whole thing, isn't it, sir? Those who seek popularity are nothing more than show-offs. Egocentrics. Not just in schools. Mondiale.'

After closing time, they walked down the Lagan Bridge Road, breathing in the cool air. Their paths divided at the weir. A mist was clinging to the surface of the river. Two swans glided by on some ghostly nocturnal errand.

'Thanks very much for all that, sir.'

'Not at all. I enjoyed the evening very much. Yes, very much.'

'I'll be seeing you, then.'

The swans disappeared under the central arch of the bridge.

Tom Griffin, as he turned right onto the Embankment,

knew immediately that they would be seeing each other again.

They often met after that evening, and as the days lengthened into spring they took to going for walks up the river to Belvoir Park or down the river through streets of red-brick houses which still preserved an air of the Industrial Revolution when rural families had migrated to the city, though almost all were now shared as cheap digs by students. They paid little heed to their surroundings. Walk stimulated talk, though afterwards Tom Griffin was rarely able to recall exactly what they had talked about, it had all flowed so naturally. He never initiated these excursions; indeed, he wondered if it was right to encourage them, asking himself if Davey should not more appropriately be spending his leisure hours among his peers – but he dismissed this notion by telling himself that so personable a young man must undoubtedly enjoy an adequate social life on the campus and that his concern with such a question revealed the pedagogue too strongly. He reflected that if he had a son he would like that son to be Davey so that they could share their interests; but on fuller consideration he realised that fathers were rarely granted the sons they envisaged and that, in any case, a son in his late teens would more naturally be rejecting a father's influence rather than engaging him in confidences.

Yet the more he thought on the matter, the more troubled he became, at times even enquiring of himself on the propriety of spending evenings with a youth of little more than a third his own age. He was not well versed in these matters but was aware that such relationships could be frowned upon by the authorities; he pictured being called into the headmaster's study and told – in the nicest possible way of course – that their friendship had been noted by certain parents and could lead to misunderstandings. During the previous summer there had been a scandalous case, widely reported in the media, concerning a Hostel for Protestant Youths where an official had taken advantage of a number of his charges in a most distasteful way. Such people were, fortunately, extremely few, but the incident had left an impression in the public mind.

The Easter holidays arrived. Davey went off to stay with his mother in the country – more for reasons of economy than for an overwhelming desire to be at home, as he told Mr Griffin with his customary candour. Tom Griffin usually spent the period writing exam papers and attending whatever staff meetings were arranged at the school. This year he also dug the whole vegetable patch in the Robinsons' back garden as a sort of quid pro quo for domestic services rendered. Yet in spite of the fact that his hours were well filled – he even accompanied the Robinsons to an Easter Vigil at St Polycarp's – he was aware of the absence of some essential element and had to conclude that he was missing his chats with young McLean. When, on the Tuesday, he received a picture postcard showing the round tower on Devenish Island in Fermanagh he was quite startled to sense a pounding in his chest as he turned it over and read the message: Bored out of my skull. Why not join me next weekend? We have a spare room. Plunder the ancient monasteries and frequent the squalid hostelries. There was a telephone number and a scribbled D.

Of course there could be no question of going on such a visit, especially without a formal invitation from Mrs McLean whom Tom Griffin could not recall having met on Parents' Days. However, he decided he must telephone for courtesy's sake and explain that he was much too busy.

The number was a land line, so he could not be sure of who would answer. If it was Davey's mother, she might not even be aware that her son had issued such an invitation. He chose his words carefully. As expected, the call was answered by a female voice – a very lively one as it turned out. He asked was this David McClean's number? and the voice immediately enquired if he were not Mr Griffin? When he replied that he was, she continued, 'I'm delighted Davey asked you down. He's fit to be tied for lack of intelligent company! I think he's got too big for Drumreask.'

Tom Griffin demurred. He had rather a lot on hand. He didn't want to give any trouble.

'No trouble in the world. This place is Liberty Hall. Will you be driving?'

'That's another difficulty. I haven't got a car.'

'Davey'll meet you off the bus then. There's only one a day and you'll have to change in Enniskillen, but it's only twenty minutes on from there.'

Tom heard himself acquiescing to everything the friendly voice was saying. Three days later he was stepping off the bus on Main Street, self-consciously carrying a tough old leather suitcase which he had found, dust-covered, in the Robinsons' attic. Davey was leaning against a telegraph-pole, grinning – Tom hoped not at his awkwardness. Really, the whole idea was preposterous – crossing half the country to stay with people he'd never met. Davey grabbed the case and they walked the fifty yards or so to the house with the sign McLean's High-Class Newsagents, Davey pointing out the 'local blemishes' and 'places of little interest', while he thought the slanting street with the low evening sun lighting the painted shop-fronts on its eastern side not by any means unpleasing to the eye.

Mrs McLean was closing the shop when they arrived. She was a brisk, lean woman with a highly coloured complexion and henna-tinted hair which she wore in a roll. He reckoned that she was probably only a couple of years older than himself. 'I'm Nessie,' she said. 'No Missus-ing and Mister-ing here: and you're, what? Didn't I hear Davey say your name is Tom?' Her elder sister, Christina, who was helping her and who, it later emerged, was unmarried and had given up her position as book-keeper in the local sawmill following Mr McLean's death, appeared as an altogether neutral image of Nessie – self-effacing where Nessie was effervescent, given to thoughtfully whimsical sallies where Nessie was inclined to deliver more spirited observations; yet they shared the same quizzical timbre of voice.

The house, which had been the family seat of Davey's father for several generations, was entered by a green door squeezed between the shop and an arched entry which led to a yard where horses had probably once been stabled. The green door opened into a long tiled corridor lit only by the diminutive fanlight. At the far end was a kitchen and a small glazed dining space – clearly a recent addition. Narrow stairs with finely turned joinery led to a very large sitting-room with three sash windows looking out over the street.

Behind this was a bedroom into which Tom was shown by both Davey and his mother. It had a view of a long garden terminating in a stand of chestnuts, their candelabra just coming into flower. Beyond this rose a tall, slim steeple. The other bedrooms were most certainly on the floor above. Tom, used to the less symmetrical architectural arrangements of suburbia, found the place very attractively laid out, and said so.

'Well,' said Nessie, 'I can only say that I like it. Most of the business people in the town moved out to new places, mainly bungalows, not long after the war – but I'd feel stranded out there. I'd miss the crack of the street.'

'The suave dialogue of the market-place,' said Davey, casing his eyes up to heaven.

'Don't be listening to that young scallywag, he's lost the run of himself entirely since he went up to the city,' said Nessie, giving her son a slap on the arm with the back of her hand and then pushing past him to bustle down the stairs. 'I hope you'll take a fry. It's all I've time for after shutting the shop and sitting down to do the lists for tomorrow, but I won't starve you ...' Her voice receded.

Tom, having felt somewhat out of place, gradually took his ease during the meal. As well as a mixed grill, there was potato bread, a brack and a seed cake. A wave of bonhomie seemed to flow between these three people. Conscious of his incongruity at the domestic board, he took care to rid his speech of the scholastic phrases and constructions which he knew must make him appear a little remote and, possibly, unapproachable. He found it easier to establish an understanding with Christina. He was less secure with Nessie, for he could not be sure whether she regarded him as a friend of her son or as her son's erstwhile tutor. When she was clearing the table and Davey had been sent out to get a pint of milk from the supermarket, she remarked, 'Davey was always saying you were the only decent teacher in the place.' He found it strange to learn that that he'd been discussed by people in a remote part of the country: so he must be viewed as a teacher. Later, when they'd all watched the nine-o'clock news Nessie rose and said, 'It's my homework time. I suppose you two lads will be going out for a drink?' – which rather cast him as a Davey's pal. She continued, 'If yous come in footless, take care not to wake me or I'll have your guts for garters come morning.' Could it be that she saw him in both categories at the same time? Or was he putting too heavy a reading on whether she saw him in any particular category at all?

'Oh the terrible provinciality of it!' Davey was saying rather too loudly as they crossed the street, making for the lighted windows of McFadden's Select Bar. In a curious way, Tom felt the years falling from him.

'And the respectability! Incidentally, isn't it time I started being disrespectful and called you Tom? My mother wasn't slow in squeezing that out of you.'

'Fine.'

'I should have been calling you that all along, but it's difficult when you've been sirring somebody for five years.'

'Naturally. And by the same token, I couldn't bring myself to say "Call me Tom" because it would have sounded so stuffy.'

'Inhibitions,' said Davey, 'fall away in the pastoral scene. Especially in taverns.'

They sat in a corner beside an open fire where the publican was burning pieces of old pine shelving which he said he was replacing with a new material that looked like pine but was easier to keep clean. Then, he said, he'd be holding onto the fireplace only for show because he was installing the central heating, something he should have done years ago – 'keeping up with the times,' he said to Davey, 'the way your mother has done in her business over the road.'

They discussed the satisfaction of sitting in pubs – though the relegation of the chimneypiece would be a pity; they discussed the popular reincarnation of mediaeval France with the novel *Abelard and Heloïse*, written by the local lady who had set up the award that Tom had won as a student; they discussed the Romanisation of Provence, Nîmes and Arles and all that, inevitably leading to Gaugin and Van Gogh's ear. They discussed the school where Tom was employed and which had almost been Davey's total life until over a year ago and which seemed to him now to have located itself in the distant past. 'That's because you're fully engaged with your university course,' Tom remarked, 'which so many students fail to do.' Davey recalled some of the members of the staff, colleagues of Tom's, who had now passed into the realm of fable in Davey's mind. 'We all thought Miss MacNaughten was a nympho,' he said. 'Did you know that we called her "Naughty"?'

'Actually yes. But it stems from the sound of her name.'

'Did you know that we called Mr Biggar "Bugger Biggar"?'

'I see.'

'Only because of the alliteration – no offence intended. "Bugger" in the sense of "Bugger that" meaning "Dammit."

'No?'

'And then there was poor Mr Bleakeley. I suppose the nickname would have been more appropriate to him.'

'How do you mean?'

'Oh, you know. Though I don't suppose he ever did anything. None of us thought he did.'

'Did?'

'Buggery. He was always flapping it at the juniors in the showers after football, but that was as far as it went. Exhibitionism, I suppose, not the B word.'

Tom Griffin could not believe what he was hearing, and said so.

'Oh come on! Everyone knew where Mr 's interests lay. Don't say you didn't.'

Tom was conscious of Davey's use of the past tense: Eglantine College was to him a thing of a bygone world, remote and half-forgotten.

'Never heard of such a thing. In fact, I don't believe it.'

'Ask anyone who passed through the school, if they even remember – it's so unimportant.'

'But – if what you say is true – and I've known for, what, eight or nine years – why wasn't something done about these – incidents?'

'Ah, you wouldn't mind the guy. We all knew he was harmless. Just horseplay. If that was the way he got his kicks, good luck to him.'

Tom was astonished – not so much at the allegation which, on account of its casual nature, was not an allegation at all – as by the disclosure of a whole ethos of frankness in Davey's generation of which he'd been completely unaware. He was not conscious of actual indecency in Davey's outrageous reference to a highly regarded colleague, for their conversation was now man-to-man; he was simply staggered to learn that there existed in these very young people so – advanced? was that the word? – an outlook, and that a teacher's alleged peccadillos could be – and were – talked about in such a cool fashion, and without prejudice. He sat, gazing ruminatively into the smouldering pine, to conceal the confusion of his thoughts. Then he went to the counter to order two more half-pints.

'You were right, of course, not to go to the authorities, but such things can be dangerous if allowed to run on.'

'Not with him. He was an honest injun.'

'You're right there. I certainly would never have thought ... I have lunch with him almost every day in term time!'

When they went back to the house Davey made tea and toasted some scones. Then they looked at an old album of photographs. They chatted on until Tom saw Davey laughing at him and realised he'd dozed off. He climbed the narrow stairs and said goodnight at his bedroom door. He undressed in half a minute and found that Nessie or Christina had switched on an electric blanket. As he floated away on a nimbus of softness and warmth, he reflected that, in spite of the startling revelations he'd heard, he had never felt so comfortable in all his life.

They spent the Saturday morning on borrowed bicycles among the lanes above Lough Erne. Davey's dog Bran plunged in and out of the rushy margins, setting snipe and teal. Davey thought he might have a swim, but, having tested the water with his foot decided it would be too cold. On the Sunday they attended the Presbyterian church; Davey declared that he only went for reasons of good public relations – there would be a grand scandale if he were deemed to be a free thinker: the Minister would foam at the mouth, the Elders, in their alarm and disappointment, would break down the vestry door and spend the money from the missionary box on gin and cannabis; his mother and aunt would experience levitation. Tom thought they would do no such thing – their feet were too firmly planted on the ground.

A traditional Sunday dinner had been prepared by Christina, who remained at home for that purpose. Nessie continued to wear her Sunday go-to-meeting hat and dark blue coat and skirt during the meal. Tom, savouring his roast beef and horseradish sauce, thought to himself that actually family life was a very pleasant institution. He looked across the table at Davey and saw Davey smiling back at him. He found Nessie was regarding him with a kind of exploratory – that was the only word – expression.

That afternoon Tom and Davey climbed to the top of Crockanaver Hill and surveyed the view over the lake towards the dip in the mountains where the Erne flowed out into Donegal Bay.

'"Adieu to Belashanny where I was bred and born",' quoted Davey. 'Complete the next line.'

'Isn't it something about "The little window where the sun came peeping in at morn"?'

'No, that's Thomas Hood – just as awful. You could make

up a whole canto of stuffed-owl poetry using lines from different poems.'

They leant on a wooden gate, looking out over the landscape of green hummocks and sheughs, tagging together lines of partially remembered verse.

'"I chatter chatter as I flow – "'

'"Dreaming of Micelangelo – "'

'"In vacant or in pensive mood – "'

'"Fomenting thoughts both rash and rude,"' Davey added, irreverently. 'Why do we have to read all this rubbish?'

Tom sensed Davey's hand on his arm as he enjoyed their compliance. When they were walking down the long grass-covered lane to where they'd left their bikes, their hands touched for an instant.

After breakfast on the Wednesday, Tom found Nessie in the shop attending to two or three customers. When they had gone out into the street he approached the counter, saying 'You know, I've traded on your hospitality for far too long. It's been so pleasant, but so undeserved! I really think I ought to take the afternoon bus.'

'You're welcome to stay here as long as you wish. And you've been a great example to Davey with your hikes around the county because in the holidays he has a way of hanging about in an aimless kind of way. I know I should dragoon him into helping me here in the shop, but when I do he looks aggrieved and says he should be reading his French books.'

'Thanks so much – but I really must be off. I've a pile of work that I put aside when you invited me.'

'Not having a father makes it all a bit – well, odd, for

him. My husband was the man who'd see to it that every minute of the day was filled – and he was by no means a tyrant, in case you were wondering.'

Tom said he wasn't wondering at all. He enquired sympathetically what it was that had caused Mr McLean's early death.

'Oh, he was like all you men – made little of the pain, but it was really that he was embarrassed to go to the doctor, which I didn't cop on to at the time. And then the cancer spread very quickly.'

'How dreadful.'

'Yes, it was. But I've a lot to be thankful for. He left a thriving business, and my sister decided to come and help me out – without even being asked. So I'm no whinger,' she added with a laugh.

Tom agreed that she definitely was not any kind of whinger. He said he wished he knew more like her.

For Tom the summer term brought tennis tournaments to be umpired, exams to be invigilated, cricket teams to be escorted on visits to other schools. The university term ended in June and Davey went to work in the bakery. They met with the same uncontrived regularity as before. Davey continued to shock Tom pleasantly with his outspoken remarks on almost everything. His perceptions were remarkably sharp.

Since returning from County Fermanagh, Tom had been privately considering the possibility of their going on a hiking holiday together to visit the places in Provence associated with the literature they both studied with such zest. He went into a travel agency and brought some leaflets back to his flat: cruisers on the Canal du Midi; minibus tours of Roman remains; holidays under canvas at sites recommended by the Cyclists' Touring Club; but he experienced a nagging restraint clearly motivated by their discrepancy in age and social position; and Davey might feel it impossible to accept a gesture that would smack of patronage.

He thought of telling Davey that it was 'in return for hospitality earlier in the year', except that that would sound excessively formal – even mercenary; surely their friendship had progressed beyond the stage where giving and taking had to be weighed on a balance. He considered explaining that it was 'a gift towards further education' – which in a sense it was – but that might appear excessively avuncular. He contemplated a ruse, such as reporting that had won travel vouchers in a raffle. On reflection, this seemed equally absurd. He finally persuaded himself that he should simply buy the tickets and trust that an opportunity would present itself for announcing his plans. He would book for early September when Davey would have finished work in the bakery and the school term would still be two weeks away.

He bought two Ryanair tickets from Dublin to Rodez which the map told him was situated on the ancient Pilgrims' Route close by the Abbey of Conques, celebrated for its Romanesque remains. The tickets remained in the breast pocket of his blazer and there they stayed while the two of them sat in Kelly's or walked by the weir. He was often on the point of producing them but seemed unable to find the moment juste.

One Saturday evening when they were emerging from an emotionally fraught Pasolini film, they stopped to buy two coffees in a sidewalk café where their paths separated.

'I've got a surprise for you.'

'You've decided to join the Trappists?'

'Something more unusual: I've decided to go to Provence.'

'Sounds like a good idea.'

'I mean' – Tom stumbled over the words – 'I've decided we're going to Provence. You see – I mean – ' He found himself stammering stupidly.

Davey, who rarely allowed himself to show much in the nature of astonishment, resembled a person in a book of cataclysmal illustrations, thunderstruck.

'We're what?'

'Going on holiday. A study holiday.'

Davey put down his pottery mug and leant back against the deal panelling. 'Alright: pull the other one.'

'I'm perfectly serious.' Tom was aware that he looked it. 'What do you say?'

'I'm speechless. Are you out of your tiny cotton-pickin' mind, Tom Sawyer?'

'Pretty well.'

'You must have come in for a fortune?'

'No. Well, yes. A Post Office bond matured. I, ehm, thought I'd like to share it with somebody.'

'With me.'

'Yes. How about it?'

'How about it?' Davey grinned widely. 'And the next question is, when?'

'Just before my school term starts. Look: here are the tickets. And the folder. I – thought I'd chance getting them without asking you in case – in case you thought it wasn't a good idea.'

Davey suddenly and uncharacteristically looked as if he was going to cry. He turned away and said nothing.

'Something wrong?'

'No. Sorry. I'm so – shattered! You see, I never quite knew – if you knew. Sorry again.' He blew his nose on one of the beige paper serviettes.

'No need to feel like that. I had the money and I thought it'd be a good way of spending it. I'd never go off on a continental trip on my own.'

'I bet you wouldn't! "Farewell Enniskillen!" and no prying relatives or barmen. Where are we going to be staying?'

'In pensions and the odd modest hotel.'

'Modest! We can loll discreetly in bed all day, would you like that?' Davey patted his friend's arm. Tom thought he'd misheard. Davey continued, 'I'm so happy. I didn't think I could ever be happy, really happy. It's amazing. I thought – well, it doesn't matter what I thought, but I thought you were just going around with me because you were, perhaps, a bit lonely or something and there was nobody else. Even when you came down for the weekend I wasn't sure. And now this! I'm a King! Le Roi Dagobert! ' He started to laugh. A couple in the opposite booth turned and stared at him. 'I'm sure they think I'm drunk. Well, I am ... And when we come back, couldn't we find somewhere to live? I'll have saved a mint in overtime and there's my grant as well.'

Tom felt his senses slowing down, as if a heavy motor inside him was becoming seized up. He examined the grained formica table top.

'I don't think you've quite got the right idea.' He was conscious that his words were being dragged out.

'What?'

'I think, somehow, you've taken me up inaccurately.' Oh but the dreadful accuracy of the words!

'You mean the trip's not ... But here are the tickets!'

'I know. Perhaps I've misunderstood you – I hope I've misunderstood you – but you said something just now about – well, I think I misheard, I'm sure I misheard.'

Davey looked grave. 'What is it? Did I say something that upset you?' He put his hand on Tom's tweed shoulder.

'I really don't know.'

'What did I say?' Davey's voice was filled with concern. 'I know – and this isn't a criticism, it's merely a fact, and a fact that's no problem to me – that you have rather, what? old-fashioned ways? But you have to understand that's what I like – or part of what I like.'

'Put like that, it's very generous of you – what I'd expect.'

'Was it because I spoke flippantly about lolling in bed? And isn't that quite normal?'

There was a long pause. 'I shouldn't have thought so. I really don't know. Let's not discuss it.'

'But I love you!'

The couple opposite got up and left the café. Tom imagined their disapproving eyes on him. The middle-aged sugar-daddy with the handsome toy-boy you read about in sleazy magzines. He hardly knew where to look. He fumbled for his handkerchief. Then for his wallet. Then he sat silently, twisting the garnet signet ring on his little finger.

The dregs congealed in their mugs. Davey said, in a

voice that sounded as if it were strained through a sieve from some distant quarter, 'Don't you love me?'

'Yes of course I do. I'm very fond of you. You know that.'

'Fond! I suppose you think I'm just a schoolboy.'

'No.' He considered for a minute. 'I think you're remarkably mature. More than I am, if truth were told.'

'What is it then?'

'Look: it's time we went home. We're both tired. We can talk about this again.'

Mr Griffin got up and paid the bill at the cash desk. Davey stood silently behind him. They went outside and stood on the pavement where their roads divided. Both looked ill under the sodium lights. They did not glance at each other.

'Good night.'

'Good night.'

Davey made a small gesture to touch Mr Griffin on the sleeve. Then they walked off in opposite directions.

Almost every evening during the autumn term Mr Griffin went to Kelly's pub, but, although he usually waited until closing time, Davey did not appear. During weekends when there wasn't a school match, he took to walking on the Stranmillis Embankment but he encountered only strolling couples, young women pushing prams and children dashing about on scooters. Once in early December he walked resolutely to the house in Jericho Street where he knew Davey had a room. The little girl who answered the door said that her mother wasn't taking students any more because the house was going to be knocked ; she thought Davey had moved out Finaghy way but he'd left no address.

Mr Griffin continued to walk to school except on wet days when Miss MacNaughten called for him in her Mini. In the summer his pupils did well, as usual, in the public examinations. Yet Dr Rainey remarked one day in the common-room that he thought their friend had become less convivial of late. Miss MacNaughten said he was growing cantankerous in middle age; he should find a way of getting out of himself, like taking a holiday abroad. 'He's like a snowman in July', she said.

Mrs Robinson felt quite stung when Mr Griffin gave a curt rejoinder to a pleasant remark she'd made on New Year's Day about the possibility of this being the year in which he would meet Miss Right. She told her husband that their tenant upstairs was not altogether as courteous as he used to be and Mr Robinson replied that if she got any more guff out of him, they were entitled to give him a month's notice.

One evening the following summer when Mr Griffin was returning from a concert, his walking route took him along the Embankment. Two young people were sauntering towards him among the aspens, ducking their heads as they passed under ivy-festooned boughs. One of the two was laughing. Mr Griffin's heart seemed to beat twice: he knew that spontaneous, comradely laugh. The couple stopped by a small gate in the paling, and as he drew nearer, he was able to confirm a familiar jacket, a dark head, an arm casually draped round the other's shoulder.

It was too late to turn back. He hurried across to the landward side of the road, turning his head away as if trying to discern the number of one of the cottages, hearing his terrified feet clattering on the limestone pavement. He rushed on, passing the couple on the other side, uncalled-for tears spouting from his eyes, so that when he reached the lights of the bridge and allowed himself a quick look back, he could barely distinguish the forms of the two young men who were so deeply absorbed in one another under the ivy fringes.

He moved on. His face turned to ash under the sodium lamps.

THE HERO OF THE VIth

The man waiting outside the manager's office in the Allied Irish Bank looked curiously like Georgie Levison. I thought that if it were indeed he, what in the name of all that's holy could have brought him back to Newtownross, for his parents had died years ago and we'd all heard that Georgie was in some fantastically high-up position in computers somewhere abroad – was it South Africa or Silicon Valley?

I hasten to say that I'm not given to approaching people who may be strangers with inane remarks like 'Excuse me: you look like someone I used to know!' In any case, if this person was Georgie, he had been five years ahead of me at St Phelim's School and I'm quite well aware that erstwhile prefects do not remember their juniors, or at least they prefer not to. For my part, I certainly remembered Georgie – who, indeed, could not? – for he had been captain of the GAA football team at school and at the same time captain of the rugby club's junior team in the town, a most unusual combination at that time. When leaving, having landed a coveted scholarship to the Keynes Institute for Business Studies in Northampton, he also won the Diocesan Prize for Best All-Rounder for he had enjoyed what can only be described as a brilliant final year as Head Boy. When he proposed the toast of 'St Phelim's' at the dinner on the last day of his final summer term, wearing the smart green blazer with the school emblem on the breast pocket, showing a medieval plough and the Sacred Heart of Jesus entwined in gold thread, the thunder of applause was clearly as much for him as for the more abstract concept of 'Virtute ac Studio' which was the school motto.

I attended to my business with the sub-manager of the branch and was collecting my documents when I saw the same man approaching me, his hand held out and an expression of benign recognition on his face. I knew then that he could not be Georgie Levison, for Levison would hardly act in so effusive a manner. Who the hell could he be? I asked myself while preparing a conventional greeting which I hoped would conceal the fact that I could not recall the stranger's name.

'Delahunty, isn't it? Long time no see.'

We shook hands. 'Yes,' I returned, 'it's been ages. – How's tricks?'

'Oh, fine. Didn't expect to see you here.'

'I live here,' I replied lamely.

'I thought you went to Canada?'

'No, that's my brother. My elder brother, Pat. He lives in Calgary.'

'So I've got the right family but the wrong brother,' said the stranger, as if this was an amazing piece of deduction. 'I remember him too. He went in for cross-country running.'

'That's your man. Given up all that years ago, he tells me.'

'And you're – let me get it right – you're a lawyer?'

I told him he was absolutely right and that he had a remarkable memory. I was about to add that I have a remarkably poor one, especially for names – as a preliminary to admitting that I couldn't quite remember his – when he said that he subscribed to the St Phelim's Past Pupils' Magazine and in this way kept abreast of news of 'the old place', as he put it. While he was saying this, I was looking closely at his face: he must be Georgie Levison, yet Georgie could only be thirty-nine at the most and this man, with his rather cadaverous face, sparse hair and (to say the least) mottled teeth, was definitely on the wrong side of, what? forty-five. I hazarded a question which might not seem too probing.

'Whatever brings you back, then?'

'Oh, nothing much. Just a look around, meet a few friends. Incidentally, I didn't see you at the Past Pupils' Dinner last night.'

I explained that I'd given up going because, one met only the people one least wanted to meet and one could meet the people one wanted to meet any day in the street. 'You always end up being touched for a subscription to commission the marble head of some past Monsignor whom you never knew, or build a new sewage disposal plant. Did they sting you for anything?'

The stranger made an airy gesture. 'I said I'd forward them a cheque for something or other they were pushing.'

By this time we were standing outside the bank, one of those dignified provincial buildings usually described in guidebooks for no reason that I can discover – I'm secretary of the local Historical Society – as 'Italianate' and which, apart from a church or two from an earlier date, seem to constitute the only architecture in our country towns. I was about to take my leave and wish my nameless friend good luck when he asked if I'd care to join him for a drink. Now I'm not in the habit of taking time off in the middle of the morning unless I have a client who feels it necessary to invite me after I have completed some case or other, when to refuse would be churlish as well as unsociable; also, I'm quite simply not particularly fond of drink, except for a glass of wine with a meal. On this occasion I would automatically have refused, but since I was feeling somewhat guilty about my failure to address the man by name, I decided to accept.

I also pride myself on a reasonably good eye for business – though I'm not by any means grasping – and the presence of a returned emigrant can often signal the purchase of a house or land, or a search into family records. I explained that I ran a very busy office with only two assistants and could therefore not stay long.

We crossed the street and went into the Butler Arms Hotel. After a polite verbal tussle, my companion ordered a gin and Italian vermouth for himself and a Britvic orange for me. I calculated that I could hardly be back in the office before noon and while he was paying the waiter, I texed my assistant Bríd Toner to say I was delayed.

'Well, here's to Newtownross and your return!' I said ostentatiously – and, I might say, uncharacteristically – holding my glass aloft.

'Here's mud in your eye,' he said, taking a deep sip of gin. We talked about changes in the town. He said he found the streets grubbier than ever, which annoyed me because

I'm a member of the Tidy Towns committee and I thought we were doing a good job. He went on to praise the city of Durban as one of the handsomest and most prosperous in the world. It appeared that he had lived there before moving to California as promotions director of an electronics corporation. He had joined the yacht club and played a spot of golf. I asked about rugby and he said there was no possibility of that because the brand they played over there was nothing like the real thing.

'You captained the team here in your time, didn't you?'

'I did. And Gaelic too.'

Then I knew he was undoubtedly Georgie Levison. I was now on much firmer ground. I told him that after he'd left St Phelim's his name had become a legend. He made a deprecating gesture which simultaneously signified modest dismissal of the suggestion and acceptance of its verity.

I bought my round, and after that he persuaded me to join him in a gin and It. I told him that one of our teachers, 'the Hoor White', had described him after he went to London as 'a Renaissance man'. (I was not sure at the time what that signified and am still not sure if it means someone who is equally proficient in maths, biology, amateur dramatics and table tennis.) He seemed pleased to hear that he'd been referred to in that vein.

It was after one when we emerged. I hurried home for lunch, leaving my briefcase in the office with Bríd. I said I'd unexpectedly met a client – and indeed I could have been right for Georgie might very well become one if he chose to put down roots in Newtownross. Bríd gave me what I might describe as a funny look.

'Three guesses as to who I met today,' I said to my wife as I sat down opposite her in the diminutive dining-area off our kitchen.

'Rory McIlroy, Theresa May and Mark Zuckerberg.'

'You're in the right territory on the last, I think. But you'll never guess:

Georgie Levison.'

'You're joking!'

'As large as life and twice as handsome. Well, actually not twice as handsome, in fact not really handsome at all.'

'What do you mean?' Deirdre poured two mugs of coffee from the percolator.

I explained that first of all I hadn't been sure if it was him. 'He looked, kind of, well, shrunk. And then, when we'd had a few drinks and he was putting on his mackintosh, I thought: that's not the kind of coat Georgie Levison would wear, more like something you'd see on an old flasher.

'Perhaps he's taken up flashing and is dressing for the part.'

'I doubt it.'

'Is he married?'

That's the question women invariably ask when they're probing to discover if an admired stranger is gay, and of course I hadn't enquired, in fact a wish to learn the facts of the stranger's domestic life had not invaded my mind. My wife's family had once lived in the next house to the Levisons, a modest semi on the Glen Road; Deirdre told me – before we were married, in fact – that when she was about thirteen and Georgie must have been seventeen she used to watch for him coming from school and then she'd leave the house as if sent on a message in order to pass him at the gate. She said he had always been friendly and once even remarked on a new yellow sweater she had put on specially, but she said was just an old thing she'd had for years.

'If he is married,' I said, 'and if he's coming to live here, no doubt he and his missus will add an element of piquancy to the social scene.'

Deirdre surmised that Mrs Levison was probably a diamond merchant's daughter or even a person of oriental appearance, which would certainly add an element of piquancy to the social scene.

I thought of the day I'd fallen off my bicycle. At that time we lived slightly out of town. It took ten minutes to cycle from our house by way of the main street and then a stiff push up the steep incline to St Phelim's. Sometimes a small black and white dog would rush out of the front garden of a bungalow and follow me, barking furiously and snapping at my heels. I found this very irritating and hoped that one day it would be overtaken by Hogan's van and its existence brought to a timely end. On this particular morning I remember kicking at it several times as I sped along. What I do not remember is how I came to be lying in the middle of the road with the man we knew as Billy Bullshit (he was the instructor at the local swimming pool) looking down at me and asking if I was OK?

I said I was and got up off the road. Everything was happening very slowly and I noticed all sorts of little things, like a hairy caterpillar creeping along the kerb, the big buckle on Billy's leather belt and the whiteness of my own fingernails.

Then I heard the strangely oppressive sound of a bicycle bell which jangled on monotonously, though at the same time I knew that no one ever jangled their bell for ever in so dismal a fashion. At last it stopped and there was Levison's voice saying in a very blurred way 'What's up?'

After what seemed an age, I heard Billy saying that a dog ran out and knocked the young fella over the handlebars.

'Take a toss, young Delahunty, did you?' Georgie was saying.

'It must have been the black and white dog,' I said.

'Head hurting?'

'No. I'm alright.'

'Why don't you sit on the bank for a while and I'll phone your people.'

'No thanks, Levison,' I said. 'I'm on my way to school.'

'Well then,' said Levison, 'we'll go slowly and if you don't feel too good we'll stop. The bike looks fine.'

I remember nothing of the ride to school but have a faint recollection of Georgie taking me in by the front door of the Provost's House and being stared at by the boarders who were coming out of breakfast. The matron sent for the doctor and my father came in the Volkswagen and took me to the community hospital where my head was X-rayed and I was kept overnight in the rehabilitation ward. Next day I was allowed to go home and told to rest for a week because I was suffering from concussion.

I never spoke to Levison after that although it often crossed my mind that I should have thanked him for looking after me. Somehow I felt embarrassed at the idea of putting my feelings into words. The following year he was promoted to Head Boy and the intricately regulated system which prevailed in the school at the time prevented anyone below fourth year from addressing the holder of the highest position, save on some predetermined matter of school business.

So I said nothing. Like dozens of others, I simply revered Levison from afar. When, under his brilliant leadership, our team triumphed at matches all over the county, we felt we were living in a golden age. On the last day of his reign we all sang the 'Carmen Pheliminses' in the Great Hall; the sentimental words, written by some long-forgotten classics teacher and often rudely parodied, seemed far less banal on this occasion and there were not a few of us who were seen to wipe away a tear.

I put Georgie Levison out of my mind for the rest of the day, occupying myself with a client in a nearby village on a knotty case of a contested right-of-way. When I returned home about six-thirty, Deirdre was upstairs attempting to cajole our two small girls into bed. She called down to me.

'Guess who phoned?'

'Who?'

'Your old chum.'

'Eh?'

'Georgie!'

I climbed the narrow boxed-in staircase. Our home had originally been a pair of alms-houses built by some charitable Protestant landlord in the eighteen sixties, abandoned a hundred years later and left to moulder away. The new planning regulations had 'listed' them, so they could not be demolished but no one would buy them in that era of suburbanisation and they remained for several decades as a mournful reminder of past altruism. When we were getting married, Deirdre declared they had 'possibilities' if knocked into one. I was not too enthusiastic, knowing the legal twists there would be with the well-nigh defunct Trust that owned them and also with the local Council if we wished to make alterations, but Deirdre got together with a trendy Latvian architect and in the end an attractive – I had to admit – dwelling was created and I was pleased that a town eyesore had been eliminated.

I started changing into an old pair of corduroys. 'What was he on about?'

'He's coming round. He asked us out for a drink and I said we hadn't got a babysitter and I didn't know your plans. Apparently he had a dreadful time squeezing our number out of Bríd.'

'Good for her.'

'So I kind of said would he like to drop in on us, and you'd be bound to be in about nine.'

'That was extraordinarily hospitable of you,' I said. My plan to spend the evening attempting to put manners on the long shrubbery that ran down to the river receded. Looking at the weather I was not at all sorry.

'He sounded quite charming,' Deirdre said, pulling the curtain gently over the window so the rings wouldn't rattle and waken the girls who had both dropped off to sleep by some magical coordination. 'Knew my name and all that. Remembered we'd once been neighbours. So we had quite a chat.'

We slipped out of the girls' room and I closed the door soundlessly. 'Did he remember the yellow jersey?'

'Well, actually no, because I decided not to mention it. But he did remember an embarrassing thing – embarrassing for me. I'd been sent to do some shopping and when I was at the cash desk I found I'd left my purse at home. He was there, saw I was in trouble and lent me the money. Then we walked home together and I thought I was made for life.'

'So he did the Sir Lancelot bit for you.'

'Oh yes, shining armour, breastplate and plumed helmet. I told my mother Georgie had come to my rescue so we owed the Levisons eighteen euro and I'd take the money round to them. I figured I'd have an opportunity to see him again but she said she was meeting Mrs Levison for bridge that evening and she'd give her the money then. There ended the potential romance of all time because he was leaving for some place in England next day.

'So instead of becoming the wife of the future President of the Shanghai and Nova Scotia Bank, you're living with a small-town solicitor in a converted labourer's cottage and thinking of sending your daughters to the Comprehensive because he can't stump up the fees for St Louis.'

She said that was about it, and wasn't I in love with him myself? And I said, 'Who wouldn't be? At that stage it's known as "Hero Worship".' She continued that she hadn't looked in the drinks cupboard while he was on the phone: 'I now find we've only got two Pinot Grigio and that very posh bottle of port someone gave us for Christmas and I was hoping to keep for a special occasion.'

I said his poison was gin and I'd better go down to

Clerkin's and get some. In the end I found I was carrying home fruit and nuts in case we were tempted to open the posh port, some plastic bottles of tonic water, a big round cheese and sundry brands of well-advertised cocktail biscuits. I wondered if I shouldn't change back into something more formal and Deirdre said that the very well-to-do don't bother what they look like, so I was to stay as I was and he'd think we owned the town. I noticed that she'd put on a black dress and her very good pearl earrings but that's a woman's prerogative and she certainly looked very enticing in them. It came to me that this was the ideal first scene for a TV soap about marital infidelities but at that minute there was a ring at the front door followed by a somewhat peremptory double knock. I went to answer it while Deirdre reorganised the bowl of fruit that I'd set out on the sitting-room table.

Georgie was wearing the same suit that he'd had on that morning and the flasher's raincoat was draped over his arm.

'Delighted you wife said you'd be at home, old chap,' he said, breezily stepping over the threshold. 'An engagement cancelled, so I thought to myself where would I find the most congenial company? Naturally I thought of you.'

If that's the kind of plámas you use to rise up in the world, I said in my own mind, then you have it at your finger-tips, old boy. Murmuring, 'We're greatly flattered', I hung the coat on the bentwood stand we'd bought in a second-hand shop and painted in Chinese lacquer red. I indicated the door to the sitting-room. Deirdre was standing with her back to the wrought-iron chimney-piece over which hangs an oval mirror which she'd rescued from a demolition site. Georgie announced that reintroductions were unnecessary as he remembered us so well from – how long had it been? – well, not so very long! We busied ourselves with glasses (as expected, he preferred the gin to the port). Though there was a hint of thunder in the air it was a fine evening so we left the sliding windows open and sat looking out over the dusky garden towards the silver streak of the river. Sparrows chatted noisily in the clematis.

'Nice place you've got here,' Georgie remarked.

'We kept the front exactly as it was,' said Deirdre, 'but we took away the whole of the back walls and added this – as you see.'

'It's the kind of place you'd pay a king's ransom for in California.'

The conversation turned to America and travel and the business world. There didn't seem to be any important city that Georgie had not visited, either for work or play. Names of well-known entrepreneurs were mentioned – people who, Georgie said, had 'fixed him up' in this or that affluent city. He had been invited to a curling party at the Granite Club. He had played eighteen holes with Spencer Tracey's great-nephew at Malibu. All the while he was telling us, in his off-hand way, of his exploits in such glamorous and expensive places I kept looking at his blotchy, uneven teeth. They fascinated me, for I could not equate them with the shiny ramparts which are such an essential feature of moneyed persons of both sexes in the United States.

Having studied his teeth, I found myself looking at his upper lip on which grew two pale tobacco-coloured stripes resembling, in intention at any rate, those worn by Hollywood actors in blockbuster movies of the nineteen-forties, though deficient – in Georgie's case – in bristle and panache. I had plenty of time to make these observations for the conversation had dwindled to a monologue, Georgie proving himself to be the kind of guest who has no difficulty at all in entertaining his hosts, whose role is made all the easier by not being required to do anything but nod in agreement or wonder, whichever was appropriate, from time to time.

Although neither of us could claim to have known Georgie well, he seemed to remember that we had all been part of a lively set in the town. When I asked him, for the second time that day, what had brought him home, he replied 'Just to make a few calls, see some of the folks.' Since no folks were actually specified I began to think that as far as Newtownross was concerned these must consist soley of Deirdre and myself. When Deirdre asked him straight out if he was married, he gave an expansive shrug, remarking that that had all been a long time ago, to which there was no possible conversational rejoinder.

Tales and reminiscences did not tire him. Successive gins were like fuel to a spirit-lamp: his energy burned brighter. I followed Deirdre out to the kitchen when, round about midnight, she had rather pointedly suggested that coffee might be nice. 'Is he ever going to go?' she hissed, making a clatter with the percolator to drown her voice. 'He's as fresh as a daisy,' I said. 'He could probably win the hundred yards hurdles without an effort this minute.'

'Not in those shoes,' said Deirdre, making loud splashing sounds in the sink; and when I went back into the sitting-room I saw that he was not wearing the style of footwear in which he would have been accustomed to attend conferences in Sacramento.

I asked Georgie where he was staying: would he like a lift? – a little later of course! He said no, he would enjoy the walk. I enquired if he was at the Butler Arms. He again said no – 'With relatives'. Then we had coffee. We chatted on. Suddenly he said there was something he was sure I'd remember: 'What about the day I picked you up, concussed, on the way to school?'

For some reason, and one which even now I find impossible to explain, I said I didn't remember ever being concussed, and perhaps he was thinking of someone else.

'No,' he said, 'I recall it like yesterday. You tumbled on your head. A dog knocked you off your bike.'

'I must have been completely knocked out,' I said, 'for I don't remember a thing about it.'

'On the way to school you kept saying "I'm alright" You repeated that every few yards. "I'm alright" I looked after you very carefully in case you were going to collapse on the street.'

'How very extraordinary. I've no recollection of such an incident at all.'

'I did you a good turn that day,' said Georgie.

Deirdre, who had been heroically trying to keep her eyes open, exclaimed, 'Goodness! Look at the time. I'm afraid I'll have to leave you gentlemen to your reminiscences as I'm doing the early school run.'

Georgie took the hint. He thanked us for such an enjoyable evening and assured us that he'd look us up again. The warm summer evening had turned to that heavy August rain which usually precedes an electric storm. When I opened the front door, a rich odour of drenched clematis entered the house.

I again offered to drive Georgie to his destination but he seemed reluctant to accept. He started to put on his mackintosh in a determined manner like Mungo Park preparing himself for the rain forests.

Deirdre was appalled. 'You can't possibly walk in that rain. Jack doesn't at all mind driving you, he's not just being polite.'

I put on a plastic raincoat and took a big golf umbrella out of the red stand – but still we didn't escape a wetting in our short dash to the car.

'Which way?' I asked, the wipers working furiously.

Georgie directed me. When we came to the intersection at the foot of Dalton Street he shouted 'Stop! This will do.'

My voice must have betrayed surprise when I said, 'You surely don't mean here?' – for we were on the edge of the most dilapidated section of the town.

'Yes,' Georgie replied, 'I'm staying with an old aunt. She would never move out of this street, you know how obstinate old people are. Some years ago I offered to take out a mortgage for her on a new bungalow, but she wouldn't hear of it. Let me out here, if you go any further down this street, you'll find it impossible to turn.'

Obediently I stopped the car and switched on the interior light. 'When you're back in these parts again,' I said, 'you must let me know in advance. If you were thinking of settling down, I could put you in contact with all the right people – house agents and so on, you know.'

'That's very handsome of you, old chap,' Georgie said. 'Well, I'd better be going. My thanks to your wife – you did very well for yourself there.'

He winked, but I thought rather half-heartedly. Then, with his hand on the door-knob, he paused and said: 'I don't suppose you have any clothes you don't need?'

There was a long silence. I actually thought I'd misheard. He waited, looking away from me, speaking at the window. Then he continued, in a voice from which all effervescence and bravado had been drained: 'Or a pair of shoes, by any chance? Or – or an old coat, perhaps ...?'

I was too shaken to reply immediately, and before I could gather my senses he said abruptly, 'It doesn't matter,' almost under his breath. Then he opened the door and was gone into the darkness and the rain.

I sat for a few moments wondering if I should run after him but when I switched on the headlights I saw there were a dozen mean little houses in the street and there was no way I could tell which one he had taken refuge in.

I thought he might turn up at the office, or e-mail me, or leave a message on the office website. I vowed that if he ever made his appearance again in any form, I would provide him with whatever legal services he might be in need of free of charge, that I would arrange for The Man's Shop to supply him with any amount of green blazers or sliotair or rugby balls or anything he might take a fancy to – in other words, I would gladly pick him up out of whatever gutter he had fallen into as he had picked me up off the road when he could just as well have cycled by, ignoring a silly junior who years later would make a pretence of amnesia.

But he never did turn up; and when I made an enquiry with the registrar of the Past Pupils Union I learned that the Hero of the Sixth had ceased subscribing, had left no address, and was entered in the records as 'whereabouts unknown, perhaps deceased.'

CATOLICA

'There's one thing I never could stand, and that's the smell of fish frying!', declared Mrs Gallagher, a guest in her daughter Síle's bed-sitting room. 'You're very good to leave the frying-pan out there on the window sill once you're finished with it, and it still smoking.'

'Och Mammy, how could I ever forget the way you hated Fridays at home when our kitchen window was never big enough to let out all the smoke! Sit over to the table now. These mackerel are the best. I get them when I'm passing though the market of a Thursday evening on my way back from work. Fresh from Dublin Bay they are. I don't know how fresh the ones were at home. Probably not too fresh at all.'

'You can say that again,' said her mother, slicing open her mackerel with evident relish. 'They came all the way from Killybegs in Jim Doherty's van and goodness knows how many days they sat in his back shed.' She paused as if to visualise the scene. 'And there's another thing: if you think I don't appreciate the idea of going with you on this excursion to Italy, it's because of the cooking, nothing else. You're very generous, indeed you are, Síle, but the food in Italy is terrible greasy I hear, and I wouldn't like that. It'd embarrass you the way I'd be sitting at the table and only picking at my plate.'

Síle replied that she was sure more normal food could be found in the hotel and she would make enquiries from the travel agent. A hasty decision need not be made. She boiled a kettle on the electric ring that stood on a ledge beside the mini-cooker, prior to wetting a pot of tea. Her kitchen was a neat arrangement of culinary devices discreetly placed in an alcove on the opposite side of the room to her bed. The room looked out on the backs of a terrace of tall brick houses very similar to the one she lived in. She liked it because there was a view of the huge green dome of the Church of Mary Immaculate, Refuge of Sinners, known locally as 'Rathmines Church', where she was a daily communicant. The only disadvantage in the lodging was that she had to share a bathroom with the other residents of the first floor but since these were all ladies, it wasn't so bad; the landlady, Mrs Brennan – widow of an evidently quite distinguished higher civil servant – had assured her that this would always be the case. When her mother came to stay, she had Síle's bed and Síle slept on the sofa.

'And another thing,' her mother pursued, 'I was never up in an aeroplane – you know that. I might be screaming the place down so they'd have to turn back.'

Síle advised her to put that out of her head and, if necessary, they could buy some kind of tincture in the airport shop that would banish any nerves she might have, and probably she wouldn't have any when the time came.

'I was always a home bird and the more so now since your father died, the Lord be good to him' – Mrs Gallagher crossed herself – 'and I've got more and more comfortable in my wee nest, with no wish in the world to travel: and isn't it a great wee nest for yous all to come to when the notion takes yous?'

Síle knew this to be true. Home, the small end house in the terrace next to the customs post in Strabane, was a frequent place of refuge for herself, for her married sister Dolores, a nurse in Bootle who introduced an additional grandchild each year, but never her policeman husband who was with the Lancashire constabulary and figured that his presence would not be welcome in the neighbourhood, and for her younger brother Paul, now a priest in Wolverhampton. Paul came home two or three times a year on a British Airways mid-week break, having duties proper to his calling at weekends. Sometimes he would bring one of the other young priests with him and they would go fishing in the Finn or the Mourne and Mrs Gallagher would provide mountains of boiled mutton, turnips and mashed potatoes when they returned in the evenings, after which they would watch the wrestling on television before reciting the rosary and going to bed in what was still known as 'the boys' room'.

Yes, it certainly was a great wee nest; but Síle suspected, correctly, that her mother had a deep-seated reason for refusing the offer of an Italian holiday.

'I'd say this room was once the main bedroom of this house,' Mrs Gallagher speculated, pushing back her chair, lighting a cigarette and looking around her. 'It's a fine room, but weren't you better off sharing with those two girls from the office? Don't you miss the company, let alone the savings?'

'Agh, I can see them in the office every day; they're nice enough but they're all for the discos. I was woken up too often with them coming in in the small hours. This place costs me a bit more but it's a place of my own.'

'Listen to me now, Síle.' Mrs Gallagher put three spoonfuls of sugar in her cup and stirred it energetically. 'Wouldn't you have a far better time on holiday with one of those young ladies, discos or no discos, without having your old mammy hanging around? Honest to God, a Sunday afternoon in Moville or Bundoran would be good enough for me – you know I never had much of a gradh for the high living. I tell you what: take a flat for a fortnight by the beach in Bundoran and I'll go down to you on the bus at the weekends. A nice type of person goes there – decent young men, settled in their ways, playing golf and the like.'

'I never said anything about young men!'

'Well,' said her mother, carefully examining a small callous on her index finger, 'you're hardly going on holidays without thinking of meeting some young chap or other.'

Mrs Gallagher had broached the topic before, but never in so direct a fashion. Síle was immediately sensible of the possibility that her mother might pursue the subject to the unacceptable point of voicing the opinion that because Síle was now approaching her thirtieth birthday, it was surely time that she take up with 'some young chap'. As it happened, Síle shared this opinion, but she wasn't going to admit that she somehow lacked the understanding of how to take up with a young chap, and certainly going to boring discos with the office girls had not disclosed a solution. In order to avoid traversing this painful territory, she decided to be almost as forthright as her mother and meet her halfway.

'Well, Mammy, I was thinking it'd be OK to meet a person like that. A very refined type of Irish person goes to Rimini and Riccione and Catolica for their holidays, that's why the flights are so popular. But I wouldn't want to go on my own, don't you see that? Also, Bundoran's gone to the dogs, I hear: it's all slot machines and IRA conventions.'

Mrs Gallagher took a deep puff of her cigarette. 'Did I hear you say Catolica?'

'That's right. The flights are to Rimini but the hotels are all along the coast.'

'Catolica sounds like it would be respectable. I didn't know it was in Italy. Mrs Bonnar from down the street went there with her sister the Reverend Mother from Carrickmore; there was a religious conference of some kind. I thought it was to the Holy Land they went.'

'I'll show you the pictures.' Síle went to the bedside cupboard and extracted a shiny brochure. There was a photograph on the cover of an immensely long beach with a perspective of coloured umbrellas and an aeroplane bearing a large green shamrock on its tail passing overhead in a cloudless sky. Inside was shown a very neat twin-bedded room with a woman standing on a tiny balcony beyond which could be seen a palm tree. A man wearing a beach-robe was reclining on one of the beds studying what appeared to be the same brochure.

'It looks fair enough,' said Mrs Gallagher. 'I suppose if the kitchen was away from the bedrooms, you wouldn't smell the frying.'

'I can enquire about that too.'

Mrs Gallagher studied the brochure at length. Síle moved the dishes into the sink.

'Not to put a tooth in it, Síle, do you know what I'd love to see?'

'What, Mammy?'

'I'd love to see you getting back on that plane and you with an engagement ring on your finger.'

'I mustn't forget to send a card to Father Paul.'

Mrs Gallagher, wearing a short-sleeved cotton dress with a pattern of chrysanthemums and a pair of white-rimmed sunglasses that she'd come across in a confessional in Strabane on the day before they left on holiday and the sacristan had said was no sin to keep, especially since the owner would hardly be coming back to claim them, was twirling the postcard stand in the hotel foyer. She picked out a picture of the church of San Sigismondo.

'I'll send Father Paul this one. He might be wondering if we'd get Mass in a place like this of a Sunday morning.'

'Mammy, you shouldn't call him that.'

'Call him what? Father Paul?'

'I'm always telling you that.'

'I call him that because I'm proud of him. You know the old saying, "A priest in the family". Isn't it an honour for us all?' She selected another card, a photograph of the tomb of St Eusebius of Vercelli. 'This one's for Rosaleen Bonnar's sister, the nun.'

It was their first full day in Catolica. The 'intimate resort' turned out to be a mile-long strip of yellow and white hotels all looking so much alike that Síle became nervous lest she, or especially her mother, would not be able to remember which was theirs. They had arrived at three in the morning but in daylight she was relieved to see the sign in green lettering six feet high announcing Hotel President Kennedy.

It could be read at some distance, she noted. The hotel lift was not working when they arrived, though they were assured in excellent English by the smiling assistant manager that it would be repaired early the next day. On reaching the seventh floor by means of an echoing terrazzo staircase, Mrs Gallagher remarked that she was now definitely in need of a holiday – but the bedroom, with its stippled saffron walls and adjacent shower and W.C., enchanted her, and it also relieved the anxious Síle who was wondering if they were about to discover something quite the reverse of what was advertised in the brochure.

Mrs Gallagher was also delighted to find a framed photograph of President Kennedy over the fitted formica dressing-table; and though she would have preferred a picture of a local saint, or better still of the Sacred Heart, which would give a true sense of assurance to the place, she declared herself very much at home – and, what was more, she hadn't got a whiff of cooking on any of the seven landings.

Having bought their postcards they ventured out for a stroll along the Lungomare. Music of all kinds issued from shaded interiors. A light breeze took the harshness out of the sun, but by noon Mrs Gallagher felt she could walk no further.

'I'm dying for a cup of tea!'

'In this heat?'

'Sure isn't a cup of tea the world's best cooler? I wonder if they have it.'

She subsided onto a metal chair on the fringe of a café. A menu written in four languages informed her that she could indeed have tea. She pronounced the word very loudly and emphatically to the waiter, at the same time pointing to the word on the menu.

'Yes madam. With cream or lemon?'

'Oh I'd prefer a wee drop of milk.'

When it came, it was not like any tea she had ever tasted. 'Still, it's a bit of refreshment.'

Síle ordered a lemon soda, which was very bitter as if someone had squeezed a lemon into the glass. 'Isn't it a wonder they wouldn't have it in a wee bottle,' her mother surmised.

Mrs Gallagher's eye travelled over the half-clad figures massing on the beach. 'You should take a dip, Síle. It's a sin to be out of the water on a day like this, and you'd never know but the weather might turn wet of a sudden.'

Síle regarded the enticing Adriatic. 'I don't know where I'd change.'

'You change in one of those huts. I see people going in and out of them.'

'My togs are in the hotel.'

When they got back, Síle decided she'd take a swim in the hotel pool and she'd change in the bedroom and come down in the lift which was now working, as the man had promised. She felt she couldn't run the gauntlet of a hundred eyes on the beach observing her pale body from the bronze security of their own. When she descended in the lime green swimsuit she'd bought the previous Saturday in Clerys there were only two figures in the water. Her mother was sitting on the edge dangling her feet. 'I don't know why they have a pool when the sea's only across the road,' she said, 'but I suppose it gives the place a bit of class.'

'You really can't swim off a beach, not properly, because

there's no depth unless you wade out for miles.'

'Do a few dives for us now, Síle – you were always the best in the Holy Faith swimming gala.' Síle recalled that she had indeed been one of the best swimmers at school, though she hadn't kept it up.

Mrs Gallagher said she was feeling like a bite to eat and she was going to investigate the cafeteria on the ground floor. A midday meal was not included in their package but sandwiches were said to be available at all times of day. 'Here, take my sunglasses, I won't be needing them inside.'

Síle put on the glasses and lay back, enjoying the sun. She wondered what kind of entertainment would be laid on in the evening, perhaps something she and her mother could both enjoy. Definitely not a disco; neither of them would like that. Then she thought she'd slip into the pool while her mother was indoors so as to be spared the mortification of hearing her exclamations of encouragement.

In order to avoid drawing attention to herself, she stepped swiftly to the brink and plunged in. Too late she realised she was wearing the dark glasses and was directly in the path of one of the swimmers.

A tremendous shouting and splashing ensued, though only for a moment. The waiter from the poolside bar ran out calling 'Ché succeede? E caduta nell'aqua la donna?' He knelt on the edge, the picture of masculine integrity, proffering a life-jacket to the thrashing bodies yet deftly keeping out of the way of the splashes. It was clear, however, that the men in the pool – the one with whom she had collided and his companion – had the situation under control. They drew Síle to the shallow end, helping her to the steps.

Within a few moments the terrace was alive with people – the receptionist, porter, the young assistant manager, several elderly Germans who had been dozing in the salone and a woman with two small children who were jumping up and down with excitement.

'Is she going to drown?' the little girl asked.

'She was only gargling,' said the boy.

'Bríd! Declan! Quit shouting unless you want a slap,' hissed their mother.

Summoned by the assistant manager, Mrs Gallagher rushed out into the sunlight. 'Where is she? Síle! Síle! Did anyone send for an ambulance? Should we call the priest?'

She found her daughter standing between two young men in swimming togs who appeared greatly concerned but assured her in English that such drastic measures were unnecessary. One of them suggested that Síle should take a glass of brandy and lie down for a bit.

'Oh Síle!' cried Mrs Gallagher, clinging to her dripping daughter, 'I got such a shock. That man' – pointing at the assistant manager – 'that man said you'd tumbled into the water. I thought you were drowned. I couldn't believe it and you such a good swimmer.'

'She's alright,' said one of the men. 'She just got a fright. Isn't that it?'

'I feel so foolish,' was all Síle could bring herself to say.

The assistant manager picked up Síle's towel and sun lotion and led her and her mother through the gathering of onlookers to the lift, leaving a trail of wet footprints on the marbled floor.

'What happened? What happened?' Mrs Gallagher kept

asking all the way up to the seventh floor, but it was not until they were safely closed into Camera 708 that Síle explained that she hadn't been looking where she was going and had jumped into the pool on top of one of the men.

'If I'd been a foot more to the right, I'd have broken his back.'

'Sure what matter, pet? You didn't and he's alright and so are you. They seem a nice couple of chaps anyway.'

'And I never thanked them. We mightn't be seeing them again.'

'They're stopping in the hotel,' said the ever-observant Mrs Gallagher, 'so we can buy them a drink when we next see them.'

'I'd be too ashamed,' said Síle. 'And another thing: your sunglasses are at the bottom of the pool.'

Next day Mrs Gallagher had a conversation with the pleasant assistant manager. He told her that the two gentlemen who had rescued her daughter had gone on a guided tour to Bologna to see the Madonna of Sancta Luca. They were members of a tour group from Ireland and they would be back again that evening. He said the Irish groups were always welcome at the President Kennedy because they were so informal. He pointed out posters announcing excursions and evening entertainments that could be booked at the reception desk. He wished Mrs Gallagher and her daughter a good day.

There was an entertainment advertised for the following evening in the rooftop bar at which visitors were encouraged to contribute items typical of their own countries. Mrs Gallagher persuaded Síle that they should attend. The first item was a series of Lombardian folk dances in which Mrs Gallagher recognised the assistant manager dressed in a colourful peasant costume and she thought one of the others was the waiter from the cafeteria – 'The dancing is to get the ball rolling,' she said. As the evening progressed, members of individual groups played musical instruments or sang. A middle-aged German gentleman in lederhosen performed a lively solo dance that consisted mainly of stamping on the wooden floorboards while energetically slapping his buttocks, accompanied on a tiny concertina by a thin woman with a downcast look who might have been his wife. Then everybody joined in the chorus of 'Come Back to Sorrento', sung unaccompanied by an English lady who could not remember all the words but was ably helped out by her friends.

After the applause, Síle was astonished to hear her mother's voice. Mrs Gallagher, a glass of gin and tonic in one hand, leaving the other free for suitable gestures, rendered 'The Mountains of Pomeroy', unaccompanied, and with much feeling. Síle was mortified to see that the two young men who had helped her in the pool were sitting in a group of people who must certainly be their friends. It could be that they'd described the pool incident to them, no doubt with humorous additions. They were drinking beer and she had the feeling that their nods and smiles were at the expense of the singer, whose voice, though certainly audible, was clearly unpractised.

Síle felt all this was too much. If she had made a show of herself the previous day, her mother was now compounding the damage; but Mrs Gallagher, encouraged by the applause, called for 'The Walls of Limerick', addressing herself in the direction of the group that contained the two young men. There was much giggling and shuffling around. The woman whose children had been so excited by the near drowning confessed to be able to batter the tune out on the piano. 'Come on now,' called Mrs Gallagher – 'and if you don't know it I'll teach it to you!'

The music began, accompanied by Mrs Gallagher clapping her hands in rhythm and calling out 'Di-diddily-dydelly, diddily-dydelly' with such bravura that she was joined by quite a number of intrepid merrymakers among whom were the two young men. They seemed to be quite expert in the intricacies of the dance.

'Come on, Síle!' her mother called. But Síle shook her head. She wasn't feeling too good, and when her mother lost herself among the twirling dancers, she left the rooftop and went down in the lift to bed.

'You'll have to meet my daughter Síle,' said Mrs Gallager to the taller of the two men as she encountered him in one of the crossovers. 'She's not feeling at her best since she got a terrible fright at the swimming pool but she'll be grand tomorrow.'

'She will of course,' replied the young man.

'She's a very good girl, though I say it myself,' Mrs Gallagher shouted as they met a minute later. 'Just a bit shy, that's all.'

'Preferable to being too forward,' said the young man as he twirled away to the opposite side of the floor.

His name was Dermot. Mrs Gallagher provided this information over the prima colazione. He was very well-spoken, she said. Although she noticed he was drinking beer, he didn't seem to her to be the kind who would take too much – but of course you'd never know with the men. She thought he said he came from Navan but the noise of the English group singing 'Arrivederci, Roma' made it hard to hear exactly what he was saying. Perhaps it was Cavan. 'If it was, isn't he nearly from the next county to us?'

'Cavan's two counties away,' returned Síle.

'Well, whatever. His friend is called Brendan. He has a kind of rash on his chin but not too bad to notice till you're up close.'

Later that morning Síle sat in a cane chair concealed by oleanders while her mother went in search of postage stamps, after which she said she was thinking of joining some ladies on a walking tour of the town's historic churches. Dermot – if that was his name, her mother didn't always get these details right – was floating on the pale blue water. Síle had a book on her knee but she wasn't reading it. Dermot emerged from the water and lay down on a raffia mat. He held a thick paperback in the air at arm's length above him. His swimming trunks matched his hair. Black. When she half-closed her eyes, hair and trunks became two black blobs. When she opened them fully she could see that his face was swarthy. Had he forgotten to shave? When he turned slightly towards her, she could see that there was a mass of black hair on his chest. Strange how some men had hair on their chests and some had none! It was nothing to do with whether they were fair or dark. Her brother Paul, whose head was a kind of auburn, had orangy tufts all the way down from his throat to his stomach, and that Father Cuthbert who came home with him for the holidays from Wolverhampton hadn't a hair on his body, she'd noticed, when they all went swimming in the Finn one August Monday.

Síle decided Dermot was right to wear black trunks. They were made from a kind of wool material and looked dry the minute you got out of the water. They also looked decent – not a bit showy like the satiny kind in brilliant colours that you couldn't take your eyes off, letting all the world see the shape of the things inside, whatever they were. Dermot's trunks were – yes, more modest, but manly all the same.

She wondered if she should stroll over to the side of the pool where he was lying but the memory of the stupid thing she had done a couple of days before prevented her. Perhaps she should just step up to him and apologise? Her mother had told her that the other man – Brendan – had said it was nothing, but she couldn't get it out of her mind. It might be better to wait until they were all having dinner in the evening and go over to his table to borrow some sugar for the coffee or something like that, and get into conversation. Walking over to him now in her green bathing costume mightn't be the right thing at all. Her mother had said he was very well mannered, so he might think she was one of those brassy ones you read about, or silly and light-headed like Rosaleen O'Donnell. She wasn't going to let anyone think she was something she was not.

Mrs Gallagher returned from her walk with a small aluminium statuette of St Ubaldo which she considered would make a suitable present for Father Paul and a string of rosary beads in polished malachite for her neighbour's sister the nun. She also bore the news that they could hear Mass in English on Sunday morning in a church with a name she couldn't pronounce and still have time to join the coach for the airport. She then exclaimed that her feet were killing her and she was going to lie on the bed until tea-time and Síle should go and take a real dip in the sea from one of the blue boxes which the assistant manager – whose name she now learned was Giuseppe – had told her were reserved entirely for residents of the President Kennedy.

Thus dismissed, Síle did as suggested. She spent almost a hour in the waves with the children called Bríd and Declan, much to the satisfaction of their mother who was trying to get a tan before returning to Rathmines.

When Síle came back to the hotel, she found that her mother's ankles had swollen so much from walking that she decided not to come down for dinner so Síle sat with a honeymoon couple who seemed to be Dutch or Danish – she could not be sure which because they spoke such poor English and Síle could never remember which of those countries was which so this put an even greater constraint on conversation because she was afraid that in opening a topic on Amsterdam when it should be Copenhagen she'd be displaying her ignorance; in any case, they did not seem a bit keen to be friendly. Dermot was nowhere to be seen, nor was his friend Brendan. In the foyer Giuseppe asked her if the evening trip to see the mosaics at Ravenna had not appealed to her and she had to admit that she hadn't seen the poster even though it was quite prominent. 'Oh,' said Giuseppe, 'you've really missed something, there's a torchlight procession and massed choirs in the basilica. But next year, perhaps?' he added slyly. Síle assumed Dermot had gone on this excursion. She imagined herself kneeling beside him in some great basilica, the aroma of incense enfolding them, and a robed choir singing a Magnificat.

'I'm very sorry about what happened!'

'What was that?'

'You know. At the pool. Last Tuesday.'

'Oh that. Nothing at all. You slipped on the tiles and tumbled in.'

'I could have broken your back!'

'But you didn't.'

They were walking towards the hotel. Dermot had emerged from one of the blue huts just as Síle was gathering up her towel and beach bag. So he hadn't gone to Ravenna.

He remarked on their luck with the weather. There was often a sharp wind on this coast even on the sunniest of days. They fell into step.

'My mother says you have a great singing voice! She thinks you may be a professional.'

'Not I!' Dermot laughed. 'The nearest I ever got to the profession was the back row of the basses in the college choir, and that's neither today nor yesterday.'

He was wearing light cotton slacks, quite tight, not all baggy like the fashion of the day, and a dark grey tee shirt.

'You didn't go to Ravenna?'

'No. Why? Was there a trip?'

'Today. I missed it because I didn't see the poster.'

'I must have done the same.'

'Apparently there's a parade and that.'

'What a pity! You have to give it to these Italians: they treat even the most profound ceremonies like a carnival. And that's where you'd hear some singing!'

She liked the enthusiasm in his voice.

'Are you stopping here long?' he asked.

She sighed. 'Only till tomorrow. It all goes so quickly, we're getting the plane at midday.'

'Same as myself. Are you bound for Dublin?'

'I am, but my mother – I think you've met her? – she's from Strabane.' She added this information in order to keep the conversation going. 'I was planning to come here later in the summer with a group from the office – I'm in the Rural Affairs Department of the civil service – but I figured my mother needed a break; she's all on her own. The girls thought I was mad.'

'Likely they envied your good deed.'

'No, they just wrote me off as a spoilsport.'

'Envy. That's what it was. Believe me, it's the least detectable of sins.'

Síle blushed. 'I'm sorry. I didn't come to Catolica to tell you my life story! But anyway I wouldn't enjoy their lifestyle on holidays. I'm a bit of a book-worm, you see.'

'There you are now,' said Dermot. 'They might be envying you your intellect or your education – something like that.'

They had reached the swing doors of the hotel. Síle spied her mother on the terrace and decided they should bring their chat to an end lest Mrs Gallagher join them and make some inappropriate remark.

'Well, I'll see you on the plane then,' she said gaily as she entered the lift.

The church with the unpronounceable name in which, as Mrs Gallagher had been advised, Mass was said in English for tourists turned out to be quite large, more like a cathedral and far far bigger than the one she was accustomed to attending in Strabane. The interior was of a pinkish marble; the congregation proved, as Mrs Gallagher remarked to Síle, that, contrary to what was often said, people do not necessarily give up religion while on holiday. They sat dappled in warm spots of colour cast by the sun shining through stained glass; hundreds of candles glowed from side altars where local people came and went, genuflecting and saying their private prayers while the visitors in the centre aisle meditated in tranquillity as they waited for the Mass to begin. 'Would you look who it is!'

Mrs Gallagher nudged Síle in the ribs with her elbow. Síle looked around furtively to see if the unseemly interruption had been noticed, but apparently it had not. 'Would you keep quiet, Mammy!' she whispered.

'But it's Brendan! And isn't he lovely-looking in his vestments!'

Sure enough, the priest who had come out on the altar steps, bowing to the monstrance containing the blessed sacrament and then turning to welcome the congregation, was Demot's friend from the hotel.

'I wonder did he bring the vestments with him or do they keep a spare set for visiting clergy?' whispered Mrs Gallagher. 'I'd say those canonicals were made in this place and the ladies who made them knew what they were at.'

If Síle had not become preoccupied with other speculations, she might have agreed, for the quite unremarkable young man was transformed by his attire. As well as this, the light from the windows and the candles illuminated his face in such a way that no one would have believed you if you said he had a pimply chin.

Síle's sense of shock was not occasioned by this apparition. She was looking around to see if he was to be joined by another priest, in a concelebration: but such did not seem to be the case. Father Brendan was on his own, assisted only by two tiny altar boys.

Untroubled by doubts of any kind, Mrs Gallagher joined in the responses, remembering her son Paul who would certainly be saying Mass at this very moment in St Botolph's, Wolverhampton; and she thought of her daughter Dolores shepherding her four older children into the church at Bootle, whatever it was called, her fine upstanding policeman husband carrying little Niamh. Mrs Gallagher experienced a glow of contentment rising within her. The swelling in her ankles had completely died down. Her trip abroad had done her the world of good. She was oblivious of the tumult which racked the brain of her kneeling daughter.

Rising for the Gospel, Síle suddenly caught sight of Dermot's face on the far side of the aisle. She felt a thump in her chest and it was several minutes before she could bring herself to look at him again: but no, he was dressed in a dark blazer and a blue shirt and tie. Brendan had revealed himself as a priest, but his companion might not be one.

'You're very quiet, Síle!' her mother remarked as they stood on the terrace of the President Kennedy waiting for the airport coach. 'But you've a right to be sorry leaving this place – and so am I. A lovely holiday it has been – I won't forget it to you.'

'Agh, Mammy!'

'I wonder will we be able to get a bottle of that grappa brandy cheap in the duty free shop, I could have it in the house for anyone who dropped in, with the foreign label on it and all.'

'You could ask.'

'Or I could give it as a present to Father Comiskey if need be.'

'You could.'

'Or I could give him the green rosary and the sugared almonds to Sister Angelica – but I think she'd prefer the rosary.'

'Please yourself, so.'

'Agh Síle, you're very short.'

The coach arrived and Giuseppe went round the public rooms annoucing that anyone travelling to Rimini airport should board immediately. Mrs Gallagher pressed his hand, thanking him profusely for everything he had done for them and telling him that he had the best hotel in Italy. Síle was stowing the hand luggage in the rack over the seat in the bus, peering out all the time to ascertain what other passengers would be joining them. The young woman with the two children clambered on board with cries of excitement.

'Any more for Dublin?' Giuseppe called into the bar.

Mrs Gallagher, festooned in plastic bags, sat down heavily beside her daughter. 'I declare to God I'm sweating.' she announced with a laugh.

Síle had her eyes fixed on the door of the hotel.

'That nice priest – Brendan, who said Mass this morning – was telling me he was travelling today, only I didn't know at the time he was a priest. And I suppose his friend is travelling too. Your friend,' she added meaningfully.

Síle was not listening. She had caught sight of Father Brendan, now properly dressed in black with a white clerical collar, hurrying towards the bus, a sausage-shaped bag in one hand and a leather briefcase in the other. 'Hold it,' he shouted, throwing the bag inside, 'hold it. One more to come! – un altra persona.'

Síle watched for the altra persona. She did not have to wait long. In the summer dimness of the interior of the hotel there was a movement as the doors of the lift opened. A dark figure hurried out of the foyer into the sunshine. It was as she had feared. He was wearing exactly the same style of suit and collar as Father Brendan.

Father Dermot climbed onto the bus, waved to her and her mother and subsided into a seat at the front. There was a grinding of gears, Giuseppe waved from the poolside and the holiday was over.

Mrs Gallagher's eyes were wide. 'And he a priest too. I never would have thought it.'

'Agh, give over, Mammy, the whole bus will hear you.' Síle gave her mother a sharp dig.

They continued in silence. Síle kept her face turned towards the window to avoid having to speak. Presently the coach drew up in front of the Departures building.

'Do you know what?' observed Mrs Gallagher as she collected her souvenirs from the rack, 'a thing I'd forgotten till today and it just struck me this minute: there wasn't a smell of fish frying anywhere we went. Isn't that amazing now? All them Italians, and not the smallest smell of a fry.'

THE CALAMITIES OF WAR

When the registered letter from the War Office arrived on the last day of April 1941 informing Mr and Mrs William Henderson that a portion of their large house was to be requisitioned 'as a home for evacuees for the duration of the current conflict', Mrs Henderson nearly had a fit. The idea was bad enough in itself but the notion that government officials – whom they did not know – were in a position to assert in writing that the Hendersons were 'deemed to have living accommodation in excess of that necessary to support their family unit', and that the same officials were aware that they kept a cook, a housemaid and a gardener – the last 'residing in dwelling adjacent' – compounded the sense of intrusion. The bald statement that 'a suitable rental would be paid, as well as compensation for any identifiable damage at the conclusion of the arrangement,' did not alleviate the insult one whit; rather, it made it worse by drawing attention to the possibility that Mrs Henderson's lovely wallpapers, curtains and covers might be tarnished – or even destroyed. The fact was that Mrs Henderson prided herself above all else on the elegance of her decorative scheme. 'Strule View' had become a byword in the town – for those lucky enough to have seen its interior – as the ne plus ultra of tasteful and comfortable furnishing. Mrs Henderson gracefully admitted that some people might now find her scheme a trifle old-fashioned, but when she had first entered the house as a bride of some thirty summers and turned her thoughts to the creation of a home that would be appropriate to her and her husband's position in society, no one could gainsay her deft choice of textures and patterns; and anyway – as she was quick to point out – good taste from any period would remain as such, even as superficial fashions changed.

William Henderson was, as the signage over the front of his premises on Abercorn Street declared, a High-Class Hardware Merchant and Undertaker. In fact, he was the most substantial in both categories in the town. He had inherited the business from his father, the elder Henderson passing away just at the time when William became engaged to the prepossessing Miss Ethel Parr, only daughter of a well-placed general practitioner in Castlederg. Old Mr Henderson had recently bought out O'Friel's, his principal rival in funeral furnishing, and when the last remaining members of the O'Friel family finally removed to Tasmania, young Mr Henderson bought 'Strule View', which the O'Friels had built barely fifty years earlier when their commercial fortunes had been more buoyant.

The mansion was situated on an eminence overlooking the river. Its only disadvantage – though it was a major one – was that in order to approach the house, one had to pass through a dilapidated and overcrowded quarter of the town; small two-storied industrial houses and shabby cottages were clustered round the vast and conspicuously sculptured Church of the Immaculate Conception. The older Hendersons had laid out an extensive shrubbery of laurel and other densely growing evergreens, to which William and Ethel added a tall trellis, against which they planted rather more strands of variegated ivy than would normally be seen on such a structure, but the ivy prospered and did its duty admirably. At the same time William had the entrance gates replaced by stout timber boards that certainly did have the appearance of wardrobe doors, but they fulfilled their intention of closing off the view of the house from the prying eyes of their numerous neighbours.

After her husband had left for work, Ethel pored over the document from the War Office. She took particular note of a postscript written in what she felt could be a sympathetic hand. It suggested that they might prefer not to divide their house, giving over half of it to visitors, but alternatively could consider taking in one large family as paying guests who would share the life of the household; the writer stated that several owners of large properties had enquired if this would be allowed and it was certainly quite in order. She rang the bell for Grace to bring some hot water for the teapot, and when she had refreshed her cup and Grace had cleared the breakfast-table she paced up and down the Axminster carpet weighing in her mind the possible courses of action.

She understood that if she accepted the scond proposal she would have more control over the rampaging of the refugees. She found she could not for a minute entertain the thought of hordes of children – as like as not from the slums of the Falls Road in Belfast, who had never seen a decently furnished room in their lives – placing jammy hands on the delicate pattern of umber acanthus leaves that was such an admired feature of the wallpaper in the lounge, or writing rude, even religious, slogans on the off-white paintwork of the study.

First she telephoned a friend of her husband in the Ministry of Supply to enquire whether he thought there might not be some other way in which they could appropriately, indeed valiantly, support the War Effort. This friend, a higher civil servant with very good connections, racked his brain at the other end of the line. He asked if the Hendersons had a barn, because, if so, it could be requisitioned as a store for munitions, in which case no evacuees, nor indeed anyone, could be billeted within half a mile owing to the danger of an explosion. Ethel replied that they did not have a barn but they had a very nice potting-shed which Billy had recently had reroofed in orange tiles. A discussion followed on the dimensions of this shed. At length, Billy's friend had to conclude that it would hardly be large enough. He promised to phone Ethel the instant any solution came to mind.

Ethel next telephoned the headmaster of the school in which her two sons were boarding, now removed from Belfast to the Golf Coast Hotel in Portrush where there was considerably less likelihood of a Lüftwaffe blitz. She enquired if Robbie and Hughie might have chums whose parents were serving at the Front – or (come to think of it, poor dears!) had lost their lives on some distant battlefield – who might like to share 'Strule View' during the school holidays? The headmaster thanked her for her generous thought but said that arrangements had by now been made for such boys – there were, fortunately, only three such – to remain at the school over the vacations, where they would have use of all the sporting facilities and where concerned relatives would be encouraged to visit whenever circumstances made it possible.

'You reply to yon letter from the War Office, Ethel,' Billy said when he came back for dinner at one o'clock, after they had discussed the situation in all its aspects. 'Be sure to say it's a big privilege to be helping them that's bombed out of hearth and home in these terrible times. And be sure to say too we'll be happy to welcome a Christian family who will observe the rules of family life. That's important. He'll know what it means unless he's a real gobdaw – though I hear they're employing all kinds now, with the best of them called up for the army.'

Ethel added her own thoughts to the letter, stating that both she and her husband, 'owing to our strong feelings of patriotism, will be only too honoured to play our part as best we can in assisting our country to victory'. She considered this, took a new sheet of notepaper, and added – after 'play our part as best we can' – the words 'in our small way'. This would remove any thoughts the recipient might have that they were a bit above themselves. She put on her heather-coloured tweed coat and a hat of magenta felt, which she knew would make no-one envious since she had bought them long before the introduction of clothes rationing, and walked down the hill past the working-class houses into the town. (Her husband's firm had an allocation of petrol for the hearse but the Hendersons were scrupulous about not using this source of supply for the Riley.) She bought a two-pence-halfpenny stamp in the Post Office and remarked to Miss Logan as she applied it to the envelope that she was inviting some 'unfortunates' to share her home; they would have the run of the house, and the garden too, and the field going down to the burn! Miss Walker was distinctly impressed and passed on this news in the break to Miss Reid the telephonist and to Mr Bryson the postmaster. All agreed that the Hendersons, in spite of what was said about them, were humble people at heart.

Ethel then called on the Reverend Samuel Hanna, Minister of the Presbyterian congregation of which she and her husband were prominent members, at The Manse. She told him that she expected their evacuees would come from one of the rougher districts of Belfast which, sadly, had so far experienced the most devastating effects of the blitz. She said she had requested that they would be of the right sort. Mr Hanna understood her perfectly and said that her protégés would be heartily welcome in the church and, if there were little ones, places could certainly be found for them at Sabbath School.

Archie Logan, the gardener at 'Strule View', was diverted from his usual duties to help with the indoor arrangements. He and his brother Ruben moved the valuable pieces of furniture which Mrs Henderson felt she could not risk being damaged by their lodgers into the rooms which the Hendersons were retaining exclusively for their own use, apart from their own bedroom and those of the boys: the front parlour and the study. The result was such crowding that there was hardly space to sit down, so Mrs Henderson had the agonising task of deciding which pieces should be removed to other safe quarters. Archie and Ruben sweated as they dragged an imitation Bühl cabinet from the parlour to the back hall on a tough length of canvas, Mrs Henderson loudly instructing them at each heave to mind the corner of the panelling and be careful not to gouge the parquet. She then directed them to try it in different positions so it would look less out of place or, as might be the case, impede traffic to the kitchen. Grace lifted six spindly chairs one by one from the study and found corners for them in corridors both up and down stairs, Mrs Henderson then moving each in turn to suit, as she put it, 'the appearance of the place'. It was inevitable that during these manoeuvres a china ornament containing three plumes of pampas grass was knocked off a low stand, Mrs Henderson crying 'Oh! my good Doulton bowl!', but there was nothing to be done.

It was decided that the visitors should have a place to which they could retire when they wished to be on their own. A room halfway up the stairs, for which a practical use had never been found – known as 'O'Friel's buroo' for it was believed that the late undertaker had used it as an office – was decided upon. Grace was asked to give a good scour with carbolic soap to a pine table and an old dresser that had been abandoned in a shed many years before and these were carried into the house and up the first flight of stairs with much panting and grunting, along with a large wooden armchair that had probably once seen service in what had been known as the Servants' Hall. All the plain chairs in the kitchen seemed unnecessary, for Grace and Madge the cook clearly needed only one each; four of these were added to the arrangement.

Archie became the hero of a furnishing afternoon when

he arrived with a pile of old dishes and kitchen mugs that he said his wife had no use for and had shoved in a box under the bed in old God's time. 'I think our endeavours have succeeded' exclaimed Mrs Henderson in a moment of euphoria. 'Our guests will lack for nothing.'

That evening she sat down with a writing pad, a bottle of black and a bottle of red ink, and two pens, and wrote out a notice in very easy words in capital letters and heavily underlined, requesting silence in the corridors, the need to switch off all electric lights when not required and always leaving the toilet as one would wish to find it. She added the times of meals: Breakfast 8 a.m. sharp, Dinner 1 p.m., High Tea 6.30. She found some drawing-pins and posted the notice above the chimneypiece. She made plans to draw up a roster for potato-peeling, dish-washing and floor-scrubbing – but this would have to wait until she knew the number and ages of her paying guests.

An unusually savage air-raid the following Sunday night sent the shattered remnants of hundreds of families from the shipyards area of Belfast into the remotest corners of the province. Some went to relatives whom they had never met but whose addresses on the fringes of Fermanagh and Tyrone spelled some sort of safety, even if they did not remove distress or guarantee any degree of composure. Voluntary workers who were placed in charge of hastily organised reception centres in church halls and school assembly rooms had suddenly to find accommodation for solemn-eyed children, distraught mothers and anxious grandparents in attics, back parlours and even, it was reported on the radio, garden sheds.

Mrs Henderson went down to the Caldwell Memorial Hall and found some ladies from Dr Barnardo's Homes organising the distribution of clothing donated that morning in a hasty door-to-door collection. Some members of the Home Guard – no more than children themselves, Mrs Henderson thought – were playing hopscotch and O'Grady Says with a group of seven- or eight-year-olds who, for the moment, seemed to be unmindful of their homeless state. Some of the children had luggage labels round their necks, giving their names, ages (if known), places of origin and putative destination. Names of parents were also given or, if not, the date and location of the raid in which they had perished. On enquiring from one of the Barnardo's ladies if any of these poor dears were bound for 'Strule View' she was told they had no information about that address – as Mrs Henderson herself found when she sidled up to some toddlers in a friendly fashion and examined their labels one by one. Most were destined for the cottages near the Immaculate Conception church – dwellings already overcrowded, Mrs Henderson thought to herself, because the people there seemed unable to exercise restraint.

As she walked back up the hill through that very neighbourhood, she noticed that here and there groups of children were not joining in the rough-and-tumble of the street games but were standing in the thin spring sunlight staring: staring at nothing, it seemed. These must be more of the evacuated ones – poor things! – Mrs Henderson surmised. Her thoughts turned to Robbie and Hughie, now fifteen and seventeen, and what it might have been like for them had they been bereft of parents and the comforts of home at so early an age. She stepped out resolutely in spite of the weight of her overcoat and the steepness of the incline, determined to telephone the War Office to report that no evacuees had yet been assigned to 'Strule View' but that everything was in readiness to receive them. She envisaged the time when the war was over and her charges could look back with a true sense of gratitude to their sojourn with the Henderson family, recalling everything they had learned – in domestic economy, for example, from Madge in the kitchen and dairy; and from Archie who would have taught them all kinds of useful things to do in the garden. Children loved simple tasks when they were made to seem like games!

Considering these things she passed through the timber gates of 'Strule View' beside Willie's cottage-orné. Archie's wife Minnie leaned out of a latticed window calling, 'They're here!' and then disappeared into the smoky interior. Ethel turned her steps towards the house and perceived three little girls and a boy attempting to jump the herbaceous border. As she drew nearer, she saw they were leaving heavy heel-marks on the trim verge.

'What are you doing there?' she shouted, her tone expressing admonition rather than enquiry.

'Oh, we live here!' the boy called, and then they all laughed and ran down the avenue and into her open front door.

Mrs Henderson had earlier made a note to the effect that evacuees should use the side door by the scullery but of course they wouldn't yet be aware of the rules – even if these were evacuees and perhaps they were not, for their clothes seemed too good: but then, charitable people had given away some of their best.

She entered the crenellated porch, to be confronted by several trunks, a hatbox, a tricycle, a pedal-car, a pram, a huge stuffed panda, a sewing-machine and a dog-basket. It was as if the last had spoken, for her ears were immediately assailed by a loud yapping. Turning, she saw a long Dachshund, the colour of something unpleasing on the road, rapidly descending the staircase, intent, it appeared, upon driving her from her home.

'Go down. Go down, you brute.' she exclaimed sharply, making threatening motions with her handbag.

The dog was followed at a distance by a tall, rather stately, young woman who approached her down the length of the hall.

'Be quiet, Hugo! This is a nice lady, you must show respect. – Take no notice, he's only doing his duty,' she said as she drew nearer, extending a gloved hand. 'I'm Astrid Sundgaard. You must be Mrs Henderson? How kind of you to have us.'

Mrs Henderson trusted that her perplexity did not register on her face.

The woman continued, 'I believe the War Office sent a telegram to notify you of our arrival.'

Mrs Henderson noticed that there was indeed a telegram lying on the console table but she restrained herself from rushing forward to tear it open. 'I got no telegram,' she declared, annoyed lest the ungrammatical phrase might reveal she was somewhat nettled.

'Well, the postal service leaves much to be desired in these unsettled times, does it not?' This was spoken without a hint of apology. Mrs Henderson noted that the woman who, at closer quarters, was seen to possess a fine complexion and a lot of wheat-coloured hair piled up in an elaborate plait, spoke distinctly, in a way that suggested she might be foreign.

'Your delightful housemaid has shown us our accommodation,' Mrs Sundgaard continued. 'It is perfectly satisfactory. We will try to give as little trouble as possible. The telegram – if it arrives – will say that the posting is for two years, unless this horrid war concludes earlier.'

'Two years?' was all Mrs Henderson could bring herself to respond.

'Yes indeed ... Oh, I ought to explain, we are Swedish. Our country, as you know, is neutral, but our government has agreed to dispose military representatives as observers in the different regions of the United Kingdom and my husband was fortunate enough to have been posted here. He is Brigadier Axel Sundgaard. He will not always be with us, except for weekends when we will all be united in this lovely place.'

'How many of you are there?' Mrs Henderson found herself asking. She felt like a reception clerk in a hotel – her own hotel.

'During the week there will be myself, the four children and their governess – a Miss O'Callaghan, who is joining us from Belfast and will probably go home on Friday evenings, returning on Mondays. When my husband is here his batman may join him at times, a young man called Kelly. I believe he's used to sleeping on a camp bed if there's nowhere else. Now,' she turned towards the staircase, 'perhaps you'd be so kind as to show me the ins and outs, so to speak, because your housemaid was not quite sure.'

'Of course. Just let me take off my hat and coat and I'll join you in a minute.'

Mrs Henderson entered the cloakroom and closed the door behind her. Two years! she thought as she hung her overcoat on a peg. She looked at her face in the mirror over the washbasin and it was as she feared: not only was she flushed but she was perspiring as well. She decided to leave her hat on because her hair was probably not fit to be seen. And of course her powder compact was not in her bag because she wasn't expecting to meet anyone ... important.

'I must apologise for my appearance,' she said briskly as they crossed the hall together. 'I had a long walk and wasn't expecting the weather to be so close. Now: up here off the little landing is the room we thought would be, well, might be – very suitable for children.'

'And indeed it is,' said Mrs Sundgaard. 'I've been in here already and the table is ideal for their lessons. I must commend you on this rustic furniture – so spare of design, and so practical.'

'I'm planning to bring in some attractive ornaments and a set of pictures reproduced from – ehm – the old masters, you know. Scenes in the Holy Land and the Highlands of Scotland and other places too – because you may find the room a bit bare.'

'Oh please don't bother, this country pottery is ample decoration. Irish spongeware, isn't it? There is a very small collection in the folk section of the Keramisk Museet in Malmo where I live. So full of character! Are these in your local style?'

Mrs Henderson, who had not glanced twice at Willie's

discarded plates, decided she had better say they were. 'Did Grace show you the bedrooms?' she asked.

'Yes. My husband and I will occupy the room looking down to the river valley – such a charming view. I think I'll put all four children in that large room at the front – it will mean some moving of beds, but I'm sure that can be done easily and it will be like a dormitory – such fun for them! The governess can go in the smaller room and I think the housemaid said there is another room on the floor above.'

'There is,' said Mrs Henderson. 'We prepared four altogether because we weren't advised of the numbers.'

'That will suit the batman admirably.'

They moved up the second flight of stairs, chatting amicably. This woman, Mrs Henderson surmised, upsetting though she appeared at first introduction, might well turn out to be something of an asset in the long latter end. It could be that she and her husband – a Brigadier! – would increase the Hendersons' standing in the town. So different from what she was expecting from the bombed-out evacuees from the Falls Road.

They entered the large bedroom at the front of the house.

'Yes, this can be the dormitory,' said Mrs Sundgaard. 'I should like the paper stripped. Heavily patterned papers can be oppressive and confusing to young eyes, don't you think? I don't believe I've ever seen such heavily patterned paper except in a Rheinland schloss.'

'I got that paper the year I was married,' blurted Mrs Henderson.

'Indeed? I knew it must have been here for a long time. And I'm sure you wouldn't mind getting rid of the dark velour curtains in what I'm calling "our" room: it's obviously a room that hasn't been used for some years and the brown adds to the sense of, what? gloom, would you say? The War Office will pay, of course. I'm sure they can recommend their own decorators. Everything should be painted white; that will make things very easy.'

Mrs Henderson said she would discuss it with her husband.

'Oh I'm so looking forward to meeting him!' said Mrs Sundgaard. 'And I'd like the carpets to be taken up and the floors sanded.'

'Sanded?' Mrs Henderson was unsure as to what this meant.

'Oh yes, with one of those little buzzy machines. It's quite simple. All these things can be done at the same time, so we'll only have to move into a hotel for about a week. Oh yes, and as to the menu – really it is good to get these things sorted out first thing: the governess will organise the children's breakfast – I know how the young things can get on one's nerves in the early morning. I require nothing more than a glass of barley-water, a croissant and some freshly ground coffee, but my husband adores the famous English breakfast. We prefer a light lunch – anything simple. Salad, cheeses, yoghurt.'

'Yog what? – I'm afraid I'm, ehm, slightly hard of hearing.'

'A home-cultured yoghurt is the nicest, don't you think? When my husband is here, we would like to dine rather late. That's when your cook will really come into her own.'

As they turned back along the landing there was a loud shrieking and barking and a tumble of children and dogs hurtled past them and down the stairs. 'Children, not in the house please. Take Hugo for a scamper in the garden.' but the children had already vanished. Mrs Henderson realised that her 'silence in the corridors' notice had probably been read, but would it avail in spite of Mrs Sundgaard's evident good intentions, and would Hugo even now be digging a hole in the begonia bed?

Mrs Sundgaard led the way into her sitting-room. 'I know the people at the War Office took a great deal of trouble in responding to your requests,' she said, seating herself in the wooden armchair. 'You asked for a Christian family and I had to say that while most white northern Europeans are nominally 'Christian', Brigadier Sundgaard and I are not greatly concerned with matters of religion. However, as a surprise, I was able to add that both my and his families are something very rare in Sweden: we descend from Roman Catholic stock.'

Mrs Sundgaard did not hear Mrs Henderson's sharp intake of breath as she continued: 'We do believe it proper for the children to be aware of the Christian festivals, though. I noticed there is a handsome Roman Catholic church only a short distance from here, with some significantly fine statues of what I assume to be saints – we must discover their names. I propose taking the children there on appropriate occasions. History is ignored at one's peril. I'm sure you agree.'

When Mr Henderson returned that evening at six o'clock for their customary high tea, he found his wife propped up in bed with an array of pillows, a bottle of Sal Volatile and a sachet of Mrs Cullen's Powders on the walnut commode beside her. She had all the appearance of one who has not many more days left to her in this world. He wondered if he should send for Reverend Hanna; but as she recounted the happenings of the day, her strength seemed slowly to return.

'Do you know what I was thinking?' she asked, applying a chiffon handkerchief splashed with eau-de-Cologne to her temple, 'I was thinking it wouldn't have been so bad if we had accepted one of those big ignorant families from the slums of the Falls Road.'

Billy said he thought the people at the War Office were probably only trying to be helpful, but the fact was they didn't know their arse from their elbows.

'My lovely carpets. The papers I spent a fortune on in Robinson and Cleaver's. My beautiful house is in ruins, Billy. I'll never again be able to hold up my head in the town.'

AT MRS MOOREHEAD'S

'We're going to see Mrs Moorehead today,' said my Auntie Muriel, who was really my great-aunt. 'She's very old, so you'll have to be very polite.'

'Will she give me a box of handkerchiefs?'

Another old lady, who had visited my aunt some weeks before in a quaking Austin Seven, had given me three handkerchiefs in a flat cardboard box with a transparent lid, so that you could see how neatly the handkerchiefs were folded. I liked the arrangement so much that I resisted the temptation to disturb their clever pattern of overlapping triangles.

'You mustn't expect people to be always giving you things. That's greedy.'

'But she might want to give me something.'

'If she does, say "Thank you, Mrs. Moorehead".'

This was an unnecessary instruction, for I well knew that there were sound reasons for being polite to grown-ups, especially old ones. I had once told my aunt's elderly chiropodist that I had liked the sweets she had given me on a previous visit, in fact that they were the nicest sweets I had ever tasted, and she had immediately handed me sixpence and told me to go next door to McQuoid's and get some more while she finished paring my aunt's corn.

'How old is Mrs Moorehead?' I asked, prompted by some

inner voice which told me that the older one was, the more generous one became.

'Very old. But it's rude to ask.'

Mrs Moorehead lived in a house on a hill a mile or so away, but much less if you took the short-cut across the fields. It looked like the houses I was used to colouring in my crayon book: there was a door in the centre with a window on either side, three windows above and two stacks of chimneys which always had pale grey smoke wafting out of them. We could easily see Mrs Moorehead's from our orchard, which was in line with its long, straight avenue going directly uphill and bounded by high hawthorn hedges. Two ornamental cypress trees stood at the top of the avenue, just where it took a little bend to the left by the kitchen garden.

We had often passed Mrs Moorehead's cast-iron gates when walking to church on Sunday morning, but no-one ever seemed to come out of them, though they always lay open. I had heard Mrs Moorehead spoken of many times by my aunt and by our yard man, Andy, but I had never actually set eyes on her, so that she seemed more like an unvisited place than a person. Andy had once told me that she had a mattress stuffed with five-pound notes.

It was a very hot afternoon. My aunt had made me wear my coat 'for the sake of appearance'. I kept looking at Mrs Moorehead's hilltop house and thinking it was getting no nearer. A full moon sat in the sky. It was quite easy to see the marks of its face, which my aunt said were extinct volcanoes. When I asked her why the moon was there, when it was usually only there at night, she replied that it was always there, though we could not see it. It had an annoying way of keeping pace with us, so that we could never catch up with it as we walked.

The road separated some of my aunt's fields from those of Mrs Moorehead. The lower fields beside the sheugh were called 'the bottoms' and in winter they were very marshy. Even now there were kingcups and yellow irises, though there was no water to be seen. A cow had once fallen into the sheugh when it was full of mud and Billy had had to send for Mr Gillanders to come with ropes and a tractor to pull it out.

I was watching my shoes growing greyer and greyer from the dust of the road when I heard my aunt say, 'Well. Here we are.' But we were not 'here'. We still had to climb the avenue. There was a heavy scent of meadowsweet. I thought I was going to get a headache but as we drew nearer to the house, I could feel a slight breeze and the smell and the headache went away. At the cypress trees, my aunt had to decide whether she was going left to the front door or straight on to the farmyard and in by the back door. I saw some redcurrants in the enclosed garden and a turkey-cock with its neck outstretched chasing a fly. When I shouted at it, it relinquished its quest and rustled its quills, emitting an alarming gobble. We went to the front door, for, although my aunt said she knew the kitchen door was always ajar, it might be better to ring and wait for the front door to be opened.

We were received by Bernadette, Mrs Moorehead's maid, who, after a short parley, showed my aunt into the front room, from which some muted words of greeting emerged, before taking me by the hand down a shiny linoleum corridor to the kitchen. Here she sat me up on the scrubbed table and told me I was a terrible weight and would I like a drink? I was hoping for orange squash but she poured me a glass of milk from an enamel jug. It was slightly turned and I drank it slowly. Bernadette also cut me a slice of currant bread. It was very hard and the currants were very black, but I ate it because I was supposed to be on my best behaviour.

Through the open back door I watched the ducks sifting succulent morsels from the edge of a dark puddle where the dishwater was thrown out. The minutes hung heavily in the woodsmoke from the kitchen range. Occasionally I could hear murmuring from the front room. An old clock with a little window where you could see the brass pendulum moving to and fro, its grey face framed by fretwork, struck – or rather rasped – four. Bernadette started making tea for Mrs Moorehead and my aunt. She confided that Mrs Moorehead was ninety-two and that Mr Moorehead had died when he was seventy, which was a year before Bernadette was born.

'Will she live to be a hundred?' I asked.

'She will if she's spared', Bernadette replied.

The ducks removed themselves to the farthest corner of the haggard, where they started probing rapaciously under a heap of old cabbage leaves.

'Searching for slugs,' Bernadette remarked.

I said I wanted to see the turkey, and Bernadette said that was alright, so long as I didn't get myself dirtied in the dunkel.

I let myself down off the table and went out of the back door and round the side of the house. The turkey was nowhere to be seen, but I ate several bunches of redcurrants and a stick of rhubarb. Then I heard Bernadette calling. I kept quiet, but when she called again, I went back to the kitchen door. She said that Mrs Moorehead had rung the bell and I was to go into the parlour to see her.

The ladies were seated on upright chairs on either side of the grate, in which stood a paper fan speckled with soot and a yellow plant in a pot. The blind was drawn down over the window, creating a porridge-coloured gloom. Mrs Moorehead was very thin, dressed in black and as upright as her chair.

'So this is the young man!' she said. I shook, or rather felt, her thin beige hand. There was a smell of camphor and dried rhubarb leaves.

'You must be a great help to your aunt,' Mrs Moorehead said.

As I did not know what to reply, I just said, 'Yes.'

'You're a good boy,' she continued.

'He's good when he's asleep,' said my aunt.

'Yes.'

'Yes, Mrs Moorehead!' my aunt corrected. 'Indeed, Mrs Moorehead, I'll miss him when he goes back to his people in the city. But I can't help feeling that the country air has done him good.'

'Good for the brain,' said Mrs Moorehead. 'That's what matters most. The air must get to the brain. The brain must be clear.'

I wondered if the air had got to Mrs Moorehead's brain,

but I felt that this was one of the things which I should not ask. In any case, Mrs Moorehead was rummaging in a little polished wooden box which stood on the table beside her. I could hear the clink of money.

'This is for you, young man.' A large coin was pressed into my hand. A silver half-crown, I realised, when I had snatched a look at it; definitely not a penny.

'Thank you, Mrs Moorehead.'

'That's the nice young man.'

My aunt looked relieved and told me to sit by the window and see if I could pick out our house. I said I couldn't because the blind was down, and Mrs Moorehead said I could raise it a few inches, as long as the sun didn't get on the carpet. I could see our roof and one of the upstairs windows and the whole of the orchard with a figure moving about.

'I can see Andy,' I said.

The two ladies continued their conversation. The dredging of the sheugh in the bottom before winter was mentioned and the repair of a boundary fence. There was also something about a bull. The ladies' voices hovered warily over the word 'bull', like birds hesitant about alighting upon some delicate bough. My aunt said she would ask Billy to bring the heifer over on Monday.

I looked at my distorted face in the bowl of a copper warming-pan for what seemed like an hour. Presently Mrs Moorehead rang a little handbell shaped like a lady in a wide dress, and Bernadette appeared. My aunt and I were shown out into the glare of the front garden.

When we reached the road, my aunt asked if I would like her to keep my half-crown in her purse.

The half-crown! Where was it?

We walked up and down the avenue as far as the point near the redcurrant bushes where I last remembered having it in my hand. We searched among the grasses and dock-leaves of the verge, the turkey-cock watching us suspiciously from the shrubbery. My aunt was mortified that Mrs Moorehead might learn that her munificent gift had been cast aside; she hoped she would keep to her chair in the front room and not look out. I said I had pulled the blind right down before we left.

At length we decided that the coin must have rolled into a drain. As we turned out of the gate onto the road I saw Bernadette at an upper window. I knew she must have seen our frantic foraging, but I did not tell my aunt that we had been observed and I thought Bernadette probably wouldn't report what she had seen.

Next morning I climbed the ferny path to the orchard, to get a better view of Mrs Moorehead's house. I had formed the idea during the night that I should visit her on my own, to tell her how sorry I was that I'd lost her half-crown. I would say that I'd been holding it very tightly in my hand but that the big turkey had suddenly flown out of a bush with a very loud and frightening gobble, giving me such a start that the coin shot out of my hand. I would ask her for a stick or an umbrella, so that I could retrieve it from the drain into which it had most certainly fallen. If my search proved to be unsuccessful, I could probably manage some tears. I envisaged Mrs Moorehead reaching into her brown box to find another half-crown. Or perhaps even two.

I looked out across the fields to calculate how quickly I could reach Mrs Moorehead's house and return home without being missed. If I went through a gap in the hedge and across the narrow bottom it should take only a few minutes. I saw two black cars drawn up under the cypress trees, and then another – more like a van with glass sides – moved slowly up the avenue. Two men got out and went into the house. Then a man came out of the front door and drove away in one of the cars. It was clearly the wrong time for me to think of visiting, with all that activity. I decided to wait until after dinner. I climbed one of the apple trees; then I went to look at the marley cat with the kittens in the byre; and then I went to the hen-house to see if there were any eggs. There was one, which I carried carefully into the house.

'She was ninety-two,' Andy was saying to my aunt. 'A fair age. And I heard tell her head was as clear as day.'

'To think,' said my aunt, 'that I was with her at four o'clock.'

'Yon wee Bernadette McArdle found her around six, sitting up in her chair, as stiff and correct as anything! Bernadette got a terrible fright. She had to run over to Gillanders' to get them to send for the doctor – but of course there was no point in that.'

'I'll have to look out something black,' said my aunt.

Next day I sat in the long grass above the orchard. Andy stopped his scything when all the little black people started coming out of Mrs Moorhead's house on the hill. One of them was Auntie Muriel. There were eleven cars and a lot of bicycles propped in the ditch. The roof of the black van was covered in little dots of red and yellow and white – flowers, as I could see when the procession moved out on to the road below us.

Andy took off his hat. I was wondering what would happen to the money in Mrs Moorehead's brown box, and if Bernadette knew about the five-pound notes hidden in the mattress.

SOUTH OF THE BORDER

'We can't let down these people from Northern Ireland!'

The other members of the Moyconlon Tidy Towns Group thought their chairperson was going to have an episode. Although arboriculture and archaeology were certainly among their official interests, they were minor ones compared to the arrangement of begonias all the way down the main street and the organisation of litter-picking squads among the schoolchildren, but some of the members did not feel equipped to host an organisation that called itself a Field Club, on its own terms – but Mrs Lennon was certainly overdoing it; there was no need for her to harangue them in so rhetorical a fashion, especially in the private lounge of the Breffney Hotel where its proprietor, Mrs Groarke, was attending to every word from the other side of the service hatch, ready to disseminate rumour of social dissent around the town. 'After all they've been through these last thirty years!' pursued Mrs Lennon, 'here they are, venturing south for the first time, and what do we do only turn our backs on them? It's a plain disgrace.'

Mr Donnelly, who was not sure if the disgrace was plain or otherwise and who liked to be sure that everything was correct, as well as correctly rendered in the minutes, asked the chairperson to give a résumé of the background to the present dilemma so that the members would have a clearer picture in their minds, and then perhaps a viable solution could be worked out. There was a general murmur of satisfaction at this suggestion from the dozen or so persons present.

'Thank you, Mr Donnelly,' said Mrs Lennon. 'I knew you'd point us in the right direction.' She took a sip of water from the glass before her. 'It's quite complicated. This Northern group is coming to visit the prehistoric mound at Newgrange and then I understand they'll be going to have a look at the Battle of the Boyne gardens. They'll be staying in this very hotel.'

Mr Donnelly allowed a faint 'God help them so!' to pass his lips.

'A well-known member of our community, who, I believe, has a business connection in the North and knows some of these people, took the liberty of inviting them to a poetry-reading here in the town, since they're apparently interested in all kinds of culture.

Miss Gilsenan, who was seated in the front row, exclaimed excitedly, 'And we all know who that is!'

'There's no reason why we shouldn't mention his name,' said Mr Donnelly. 'We're all friends here, but we should withhold his name from the minutes.'

Mrs Lennon took the point. 'Well, I did think it was a bit forward of Mr Braithwaite taking that on himself. And what committee exists in the town to organise such an event but ourselves? We've no experience in that line but we'd have to pull out all the stops so as not to let down the side, if you see what I mean. Then, at our last meeting, which I heard was very badly attended owing to the camogie finals, which I had to be present at myself, it was decided we wouldn't have anything to do with the northern visitors due to pressure of work, as if that would solve the problem. I thought that was very inhospitable, knowing what these visitors are coming from.' The chairperson looked as if she might be on the verge of sustaining another outburst.

'Oh goodness, Maisie, don't we all know that Mr Braithwaite will organise the poetry himself, and it's he will do the readings,' exclaimed Miss Gilsenan.

'No doubt of that,' replied the chair. Isn't he a dab hand at it given years of experience, but when the final poem is recited out loud for all to hear what do the visitors do then? Where will they go? Walk down the street and admire the flowerpots at the Market House, I suppose?'

Miss Gilsenan enquired what was the precise function of a Field Club, because she felt at a bit of a loss. The chair replied that it was scientific, embracing general culture but chiefly to do with the study of nature: this she'd read on some leaflet that had come her way. 'The Field Clubs were quite a popular movement in Victorian times, I learn. They used to go on hikes to places like Stonehenge and the Kyles of Bute. I suppose you could say they were naturalists.'

'That wouldn't be confused with nudists, would it?' asked Miss Gilsenan naughtily.

There was some laughter, which the chair ignored. Miss Trench-Farren raised her hand. 'As these people appear to be interested in antiquities, among other things, I think I could arrange for them to visit Ballycloran – it is one of the very oldest houses in the county, if not the country, and of course there's the remains of the Norman tower in the grounds. Couldn't we rustle up a picnic snack or something that wouldn't cost too much? I do agree it would be very bad form indeed were we to give them a cold shoulder, and the gentleman just mentioned could read his poems there – in the garden, perhaps, or if the weather were inclement, in the drawing-room.'

'Through the chair: since they appear to come from Larne, their expectations can't be too high,' remarked Mr Donnelly.

'That's where you're wrong,' returned the chair, 'people who come from that kind of manufacturing meelyew always have very high expectations indeed. Well,' she resumed after a second's pause for this to sink in, 'shall we say – for the minutes – that we heartily welcome our visitors from Northern Ireland and a programme will be devised to show off the best aspects of our heritage?' And in the meantime we'll do our best to make suitable arrangements – though honest to God,' she continued in her off-the-record voice, 'I hope we won't be seen to be making eejits of ourselves.'

Amoelia Trench-Farren drove her little Ford carefully up the rutted avenue of Ballycloran House. She had known its owner, Bobsy Skryne, for sixty years. They had been neighbours as children, not liking each other much, she describing him as a chinless wonder, he describing her as likely to turn into a horse before his very eyes; when the age came for attendance at local hunt balls, which neither of them enjoyed, they took refuge in each others' company. Bobsy proceeded to London where he found a position as a porter at Sotheby's from which he was never promoted. Amoelia went to Welwyn Garden City where she trained as a hospital almoner, at which she performed so diligently she was placed in charge of the entire pool of almoners, employed by the Herts County Health Alliance. She retired at sixty-five to her old home in County Meath, dividing the house judiciously into two sections and renting the half that she did not occupy herself to holiday-makers. He, to his immense surprise – and, indeed, pride – inherited Ballycloran when his cousin, Geoffrey de la Poer Skryne, died from the bite of a cobra in Kerala while filming a natural-history programme for the BBC. Amoelia kept urging Bobsy to divide his house in the way she had done, 'as a certain money-maker', but somehow he never got round to it, stating, when questioned, that it would destroy the unity of the seventeenth-century design.

Amoelia drew up in front of the granite portico of Ballycloran, noting that the gravel was somewhat weedy – this would have to be dealt with. She mounted the five steps to the glazed doorway, turning to admire the fine stand of trees which only partially obscured the top of the medieval tower-house. She pressed the electric bell and when there was no response she banged the knocker (it definitely required a touch of brass polish) quite loudly and sharply. Presently through the smoked glass she noted a figure pulling up his trousers as he approached the doorway.

'Oh it's you is it, you awful old trout,' Bobsy exclaimed, wrenching the door open with a rasping sound.

'It is indeed. Compliments pass when the quality meet, I always say. How are you, you silly old faggot? It's too long since we uncorked a bottle together, we've much to talk about. I brought you this bottle of Amritzo, it's advertised as "the Irish port" but I hear it's quite nice. Grown on the sun-drenched slopes of the Slieve Bloomers, I dare say.'

She took the bottle out of a supermarket bag and handed it across the threshold.

'Come in, come in. Any port in a storm,' replied Bobsy, repeating a time-honoured quotation. They went through the door at the back of the hall to the little room that Bobsy kept as his study, referring to it as his 'den' when he wished to be understood as being a person of consequence who would brook no nonsense. He produced glasses from a cupboard next to the chimneypiece, in which burned a one-bar electric heater. They toasted each other with mock formality, Bobsy remarking that it was 'Not bad at all', which surprised Amoelia because she had bought it from among an array of special offers on a stand near the hardware counter.

After the best part of an hour, during which Bobsy helped himself to several refills of port and they had discussed the unfair rise in income tax, the high cost of living per bottle and the state of the American presidency, almost setting that nation to rights, Amoelia broached her topic. 'You're going to be at the centre of a most important event in the cultural life of this neighbourhood, Bobsy. No one will do so with more aplomb than you.'

'Oh really?' returned Bobsy, flicking cigarette ash into the empty fireplace behind the heater.

Amoelia outlined the dilemma that was perplexing the local committee. A group of very important people from Northern Ireland, she said, would be visiting the area, and a local resident – without so much as a by-your-leave! – had taken it upon himself to invite them to a session of Irish poetry, which he would select and read himself. The committee was looking for an attractive and interesting venue for this to take place, and it was their unanimous hope that Bobsy would provide that place. 'It's so lovely here,' Amoelia continued. 'You may not think so yourself because you're so familiar with it but really I think you've a duty to let important people admire this place for a couple of hours.'

'It is pretty good, isn't it?' said Bobsy. 'I often think of opening it to the public permanently but I don't seem to get anywhere with my ideas. You know Swift went to school here? It was a private school for a time in the early eighteenth century.'

'I did know that,' said Amoelia, 'though I wasn't aware that Swift was one of the pupils.'

'Oh yes, but he went to England at the age of twelve. And of course I could show these people the propeller.'

'Propeller?'

'My great-uncle Barney built a light aircraft in the hayshed some years after the end of World War Two. I never met him of course, but he was said to have been a bright young chap. The propeller survived. In fact I brought it inside and fixed it up in the back hall with rawlplugs.'

Amoelia said she thought things like that would make their day because they led such a dull existence up there in the North. 'And let's hope our friend reads some jolly poems, though I don't imagine there's much hope of that.'

'I have some limericks I could recite.' Bobsy paused. 'But perhaps not if there are any ladies present.'

'Unfortunately there will be more ladies than gents, it's always that way. The reader will be a Mr Braithwaite; he's a businessman in the town.'

'The name rings a bell,' said Bobsy. 'Is he remotely associated with wax polish, something like that?'

'Quite right, but not remotely. In fact, he's the manager of Saorstát Solvents. He came here from the parent company in Dagenham which was enticed by a government grant. None of us thought it would last a year, or even a month, but Mr Braithwaite is a nifty operator, I will give him that, and before long they were exporting all over the known world – and probably to other places too. We all thought Mr Braithwaite was an asset to the town and I suppose he is. He has a pretty wife and five lovely little girls – but then he started reading Irish literature and nothing would stop him organising verse-speaking contests that always ended up with him reading some selections from Yeats or whomever his latest discovery was – oh yes, other Irish poets who we'd never even heard of.'

'How perfectly frightful!'

'Oh yes, quite ghastly, but that's why we think this particular reading should be held here, so as the visitors can be admiring the view and letting their imaginations wander round the old buildings.'

'Couldn't you just give this bloke the kibosh and send him packing?'

'A very sensible and pertinent suggestion, Bobsy, and one that is entirely worthy of your sensitive nature: but the position requires a very subtle approach because this same Mr Braithwaite subscribes to our magazine; in fact he pays the production costs of every issue.'

'It always ends up the same way with the English, doesn't it?' remarked Bobsy thoughtfully. 'They take over everything and in the end they have to be got out.'

'Oh yes, but the difficulty is to know when the right moment comes for the push.'

'Put another way,' said Bobsy, 'the Engish are really as foreign as Hottentots.'

Cuckoos cuckooed. A corncrake craked. It was a perfect summer day. When the members of the committee arrived at Ballycloran they were relieved to see that the forecourt had been scuffled and the grass mown, probably for the first time in several years. On closer inspection it was seen that cattle had been in the habit of grazing there and had left the imprint of their hoofs in the sward so that the front lawn could hardly be pointed out to the visitors as one of the chief glories of the property. Mrs Lennon, however, had managed to gather a dozen or so brightly coloured rugs, which, when placed apparently at random on the worst spots, did not look too bad at all – in fact they lent an air of mild festivity – 'quite like *Déjeuner sur l'herbe*', as Amoelia Trench-Farren remarked when she arrived, her car crammed with apple tarts and sponge cakes that she had requested with humorous threats from a number of her neighbours. Members of the committee had been abjured to 'hold back' from these delicacies since there would barely be enough to go round the visitors.

Amoelia's cousin, a tiny lady with a faraway look, seemed to be in charge of the refreshments which she was unloading carefully from the back seat. Known severally in the neighbourhood as 'Miss Trench-Farren's housekeper', 'the unpaid servant' and 'the poor relation', Cousin Mildred enjoyed occasions of this kind enormously.

It had been decided that the poetry reading would take place at the sundial. Mr Donnelly had asked Bobsy if he might arrange some of the handsome dining-room chairs – 'weather permitting of course!' – in a semi-circle, 'for the VIPs', he had added, 'of which you'll be the principal one', and Bobsy had readily agreed. 'I'll sit in the centre,' he said. Fortunately, there was adequate time for making these arrangements since the visitors had indicated that they would be attending matins in St Feichin's – how they had discovered the local Protestant church certainly showed admirable organisational ability, Mr Donnelly thought; indeed, they may have been using one of these new electronic gadgets to suss the joint in advance. When scrubbing the top of the sundial with a handful of grass to remove the bird droppings, Miss Gilsenan inadvertently dislodged the shadow flange; since it refused to remain upright, she quickly concealed it in a neighbouring rhododendron, while thinking that without the flange, the top of the sundial would provide a much better rest for books; she could confess her little misadventure later in the day.

Bobsy Skryne soon appeared on the front steps dressed in very wide cricket flannels and a smart blue and orange striped blazer, his hair plastered down with some kind of lotion. He summoned the members of the committee into the house 'for a quick nip: some plum brandy I've just received as a belated birthday-present from a nephew in Turkey – pleasant young bloke, I'm sure he knows he'll be inheriting this place when I'm dead and gone. And I had some of the village wallahs round yesterday to give the place a bit of a tidy-up and I can tell you I wouldn't have wasted this bottle on them had it arrived – but I did treat them to a crate or two of beer in the kitchen in case you think I was being mean.'

Amoelia thought the place looked surprisingly well – partly owing to the sunshine, of course. If the wallpapers were somewhat discoloured and the fabrics faded, the furniture itself was nothing short of magnificent. She left the gathering in the morning-room and made a tour of the house, pulling Nottingham blinds down over the top half of the windows to create a mellow light. She opened one or two a crack at the bottom hoping that some bluebottles that were making noisy explorations of the rooms would sense the fresh breeze and make their departure. She found a mummified magpie on the drawing-room hearthrug and kicked it under the flounce of a settee.

Entering the stone-flagged basement kitchen, she saw that the village wallahs had indeed been present the previous evening for there were empty stout and whiskey bottles on, beside and under the long deal table. Who had supplied the whiskey? she wondered. Could it have been Bobsy himself, though he hadn't referred to it – but any excuse for an expensive nip ... There was also a profusion of unwashed glasses, mugs, cups and (it appeared) vases. She decided that the members of the Larne Field Club should not be allowed down to the kitchen quarters but rather steered up the back staircase to admire the Victorian porcelain WC which was decorated in a pattern of wild gentians and which

Bobsy had frequently threatened to have removed and dispatched to his former place of employment for sale – but this he had never quite got round to accomplishing. The teas and coffees could be served from the pantry next to the dining-room and she'd set Cousin Mildred to this task.

Amoelia emerged onto the front steps to find the other members of the committee already there, having been summoned by a tremendous beeping as Mr Braithwaite approached in his BMW. He, his wife and five daughters emerged from the car, some of them carrying books. Mrs Lennon and Miss Gilsenan came down the steps to receive them and to explain that the reading would take place at the sundial. 'Indeed,' said Mrs Lennon, 'we've set out these beautiful chairs so as your hearers will be comfortable, and the rest of us will recline on the rugs.'

Mr Braithwaite seemed quite pleased. His family followed him to the sundial and helped him to sort his papers, which his daughters would hand to him one by one as he read. He made a little pile of books on the grass.

'I hope to God he isn't going to read his way through that lot,' muttered Mr Donnelly. 'If he is, we'll be here till Christmas.'

'It's out of our hands,' replied Mrs Lennon in a fatalistic tone.

At this moment a dark blue minibus, bearing the legend Ulsterbus, was seen approaching the house very slowly as if its driver was making a point of avoiding every pothole. The members of the committee made for the steps so as to welcome the visitors as they climbed out of the van, smoothing their clothes, the men in navy or brown suits, the women in neat coats and skirts.

'I suppose we should have done better,' said Mr Donnelly, who was wearing jeans and a tee-shirt.

'Nonsense,' said Mrs Lennon, 'they'll think we're being informal and welcoming. Which we are.' She left his side and walked towards the minibus with her hand outstretched. 'I'm Bríd Lennon,' she said. 'You're all very welcome to Ballycloran!'

Greetings were exchanged. There appeared to be seven members of the Field Club, plus their driver. Amoelia was relieved that she had brought enough cups, which Cousin Mildred would by now have set out in the dining-room. It seemed that the visitors wished to take some photographs before seating themselves for the reading. This they did, snapping each other, their minibus and its driver, who was addressed with much laughter as Duncher.

Eventually Mrs Lennon was able to shepherd the party to the lawn where Mr Braithwaite was waiting with a somewhat impatient look on his face and most members of the local committee were already reclining on the rugs. At this moment Cousin Mildred appeared on the steps to announce 'We forgot the milk!' – an annoying moment for Amoelia for she would have to go home in the car; but it also meant that she wouldn't have to sit through Mr Braithwaite's recital. As she was leaving, she noticed that, when sat upon the Hepplewhite chairs slowly sank in the moist turf, 'up to their mahogany hocks' as she later recalled the scene, but it was clear that everyone was being very polite, pretending not to notice.

Mr Braithwaite announced in the queremonious tones of Cheshire that he was going to talk about the literary associations of Ballycloran – a surprise subject and possibly more interesting than a reading. The local members of his audience took notice, for they were none of them aware of associations of any such kind. 'The most notable visitor here was the famous Irish poet Yeets,' Mr Braithwaite informed his audience. 'Yeets stopped here for a night in 1897, or it may have been 1907 – opinions differ on these scholarly matters. He composed a poem in one of the bedrooms.'

'I didn't know that!' exclaimed Bobsy from his sunken seat. 'How interesting!'

'It was long before you came to live here,' returned Mr Braithwaite, pleased that he was making an impression at so early a stage. 'The poem was called "The Hosting of the Siddy".'

'What the hell is he raving about?' Mr Donnelly asked Miss Gilsenan under his breath.

Miss Gilsenan was suppressing a fit of giggles. 'He doesn't know how to pronounce Sidhe,' she whispered.

Mr Braithwaite read the poem. During the round of applause, Miss Gilsenan said their visitors probably thought the poem was called 'The Hosting of the City' because people from the North pronounce City with a d, like Americans.

Mr Braithwaite was in full flight. 'The playwright and biographer Richard Brinsley Sheridan came from these parts. His father and grandfather were local people.'

'My mother was a Sheridan!' announced Bobsy.

'Well there you are!' Mr Braithwaite performed a gracious bow in Bobsy's direction. 'I do not know if Sheridan wrote *The School for Scandal* here or in some other place, but he may have written *The Life of the Rev. Dr. Dean Swift* here because, as you know, Swift had associations with the neighbourhood too.'

'He's getting his generations a bit mixed up,' murmured Miss Gilsenan.

'I am now going to read you a passage from *Gulliver's Travels.*' One of Mr Braithwaite's daughters, a lady of some twenty or thirty summers, handed her father a large, colourful volume bearing the subtitle 'Illustrated from the Walt Disney motion picture'. The audience sat in apparent delight as they listened to this account of the adventures of Lemuel Gulliver in the Land of Laputa. Mrs Lennon realised that the warmth of the sun, the pleasant summer breeze and the sound of wood-pigeons conversing in a sycamore created a feeling of contentment, never mind the inaccuracies of the speaker.

'It's even better than *Snow White*, isn't it?' posited Mr Braithwaite, to mild applause. He then read a selection of poems by the late Fred Higgins who, he said, had brought the County Meath into literary favour in the early twentieth century.

'At least he's right there,' Mr Donnelly said in an undertone.

The selection of Meath poems did go on for rather a long time, however. During its course, Amoelia returned with the milk and she and Cousin Mildred put the finishing touches to what was to be described as 'a snack'. She signalled to Mrs Lennon from the steps to the effect that the reading should be drawn to a close. Mrs Lennon rose from her rug and was seen to make a number of attempts to start thanking Mr Braithwaite without being seen to interrupt him, but his eyes seemed glued to his notes. It was only when a sudden gust of wind – was the day going to turn nasty? – flicked the papers from the top of the sundial that he came to a sudden stop. He looked uncharacteristically non-plussed and Mrs Lennon took the opportunity of gracefully thanking him for his knowledge and scholarship, moving on to welcome the members of the Larne Field Club, 'from the distant glens of Antrim'.

An elderly gentleman in a dark grey suit rose with some difficulty from his chair, returning thanks. He said the club had never been down south before and he hoped that this visit would be duplicated in the opposite direction before long. Mrs Lennon then announced that light refreshments were available in the dining-room, courtesy of Mr Skryne: whereupon Bobsy called out, 'Oh no! We must do the tour of the house first. I'll be your guide. Follow me.'

He led the way through the front hall, climbing onto the library table the better to be seen and heard. Most of the local people had never been in the house before. They eased their way to the front of the room so as to be sure of hearing whatever gems of history the eccentric Mr Skryne would come out with, and eager to learn the provenance of certain paintings and pieces of furniture that would, inevitably, come up for auction in the not too distant future.

'That spear hanging over the mantlepiece was snatched in timely fashion by my great-great-grandfather, Beauchamp Skryne, from the grasp of a Pathan who looked as if he was up to no good.' said Bobsy. 'One jab of that article and you're a gonner.'

'Gracious me!' exclaimed Cousin Mildred. 'What happened to the Pathan?'

'Oh I expect Beauchamp had him stuffed,' replied Bobsy. 'Now, this magnificent tiger skin is from a later generation. A maternal great-uncle came face to face with him outside his tent and shot him before breakfast.'

Cousin Mildred, on tipoe, her chin barely a foot or so above the edge of the table, was entranced. 'Was that here?' she asked.

'No,' replied Bobsy without demur. 'It was about fifty miles north of Rangoon.'

There were many bound volumes of *Punch* on the shelves, Bobsy said, and also sets of first editions of Dickens and Thackeray, but he had never had time to read them. Asked by one of the visitors from Larne what painter had executed the landscape with cattle grazing in the foreground, he admitted that he had no idea – 'But it's always been there, and I like it ... Now, if you'll move on to the back hall, we'll have a decko at the propeller.'

There was much good-natured jostling among the members of the committee, though the visitors appeared somewhat bemused; perhaps they were wanting their lunch. It was rather dark in the back hall. Bobsy pressed the light switch. There was a loud fizz and a bulb suspended in a marbled bowl flashed and then turned black.

'These damned modern fittings,' remarked Bobsy. 'Well, you can see the propeller well enough; there's not much to a propeller, is there? That wooden boyo on the wall is one, in fact it's the propeller of an aircraft that my great-uncle built in the nineteen twenties. It was definitely built here,' he said, gallantly addressing Cousin Mildred, 'in case you were wondering.'

'Oh I was, I was!'

'My Uncle Edgar was said to have had a flair for engineering, especially aeronautics. He designed this flying-machine on the principle of the catapult, apparently borrowing the idea from Leonardo da Vinci. It was his plan to fly to Dublin and land at the Horse Show.'

'And what did the people at the Horse Show say when they saw the flying machine?' asked Cousin Mildred.

'Well, actually, he never got there. There were technical difficulties. First he had to raise the machine to the top of the old tower so that it would start its flight with height already attained. This was achieved by means of a dozen horses pulling on ropes. I'm told that the plane looked most impressive sitting on the top of the tower, like an eagle on its eyrie. Then Uncle Edgar decided that it would be better if his handyman, Pat Langan, piloted the test flight. Pat had worked for two years on the project and knew the machine inside-out, you see. So Pat climbed into the cockpit and two blindfolded horses wound up the catapult. Uncle Edgar shouted 'Cast off!' – but something must have gone wrong because the plane fell into the herbaceous border.'

'And what happned to Pat?' Cousin Mildred was agog.

'I expect they carted him off to the county infirmary.'

Mrs Lennon's eye had spotted a small chiffonier which she thought would look well in her sitting-room. She imagined herself approaching Bobsy at a later date and asking would he consider parting with it; indeed, what did he live on? she wondered – surely not the state pension? He might welcome a discreet sale. She decided to start her campaign now.

'What a pretty piece of furniture,' she exclaimed. 'Do tell us its history!'

'It's an heirloom,' Bobsy replied. 'It goes back centuries. I believe It came from Versailles.'

'I think you must be mistaken,' Amoelia interposed, summoning with difficulty a light-hearted tone of voice. Really Bobsy was going beyond himself. 'Your mother, as I recall, bought it at my mother's residual sale. She said she'd admired it all her life and purchasing it would be a nice finale to their friendship. Sorry for correcting you.'

'Oh not at all,' said Bobsy, 'but I do think it originally belonged to Marie Antoinette.'

'Well perhaps it did,' Amoelia conceded; 'it does have a kind of French look.' To her dismay, Bobsy led his visitors down the basement steps. 'This is the old kitchen,' he said, opening the door on the remains of what had the appearance of a drunken orgy. Well, Amoelia thought, it's his house not mine.

She expected their guests to snigger, but none of them did, merely appearing astonished, as if suddenly confronted by some celebrated work of conceptual art. Photographic flashes pierced the gloom like bolts of lightning in the underworld.

'In my grandparents' time there used to be a cook-general, two kitchen-maids, a parlourmaid, a butler and a pantry-boy,' Bobsy recalled.

An Ulster voice was heard to observe that there must have been several pantry-boys last night.

Gradually the crowd moved to the dining-room where the light refreshments were availed of. Two of the visitors strode purposefully outside with their cameras, spending some time photographing the trees that stood between the mansion and the remains of the tower. 'Remarkable specimens!' one of them declared when joined by Bobsy and Mrs Lennon, who were preparing to deliver their farewell remarks.

'When were they collected?' the taller of the two enquired.

'Collected?'

'Yes. From California. I assume they were brought here for planting by a forebear of yours – or do you think the seeds were purchased from Kew? The eighteen sixties I should think. '

'I've no idea,' replied Bobsy, not in the slightest bit ashamed about his lack of knowledge of family history. 'They've always been here.'

'They are about the finest sequoia sempervirens I've ever seen!' asserted his visitor.

'Would you say so?' replied Bobsy ruminatively. 'Yes, I always thought they were something.'

The participants gathered about the minibus to shake hands and exchange suitable words of farewell. A Miss McGivern, who identified herself as Honorary Secretary of the Field Club, said it had been a day they would all remember. 'We have taken many photographs and they will appear in our Annual Report as a lasting memento of our visit,' she promised. 'I would also like to add that if any of you ever wish to visit Larne, I can guarantee a warm welcome. There is much of interest apart from our club's activities. We are a highly industrialised community and we can take you on a tour of our power station, our chemical plant and our rayon factory which is the largest in the United Kingdom.'

'How divine,' breathed Cousin Mildred.

In due course Miss McGivern, a sociologist by profession, read an interesting paper to the members of the Larne Field Club on the subject of rational decline in certain enclosed societies of Southern Ireland. In response to questions she added that this was clearly the result of inbreeding, an inordinate consumption of alcoholic beverages and an absence of contact with more advanced societies. The members of the Moyconlon Tidy Towns Group were unaware of this but they were horrified when Mr Braithwaite passed them a complimentary copy of *The Larne Naturalist* in which there were not only some superb photographs of the Californian redwoods at Ballycloran but also – fortunately without captions other than the teasing 'After the Ball was Over', a picture of a basement kitchen liberally decorated with empty bottles and another showing a person who could only be Cousin Mildred attempting to climb onto a Sheraton sideboard for a closer view of the Pathan's spear; it was entitled 'Let me see too!'

'Those people are really savages at heart!' the Chairperson said of their Northern visitors at the next meeting of her committee. 'We may not care to admit it, but the people of our north-eastern province have a world-wide reputation, I'll only say reputation, which they always manage to live up to.'

'Not for the minutes,' Mr Donnelly added.

'Oh no, not for the minutes, unfortunately.'

Amoelia Trench-Farren decided to have copies of the tree photographs made for Bobsy Skryne, to emphasise the fact that the effort he had put into the day at Ballycloran had been really worthwhile. She delivered them one Sunday afternoon when the daffodils were coming into expansive flower on his lawn.

Bobsy thought the pictures were quite good – 'But,' he said, 'I can always look at the trees as they are. I don't need photographs. And I don't need to know they are Californian Whatsits; they're just my trees. Come inside and join me in a wee nip.'

They went into his den where a bottle of Jameson Seven was already open on the sandalwood escritoire. 'One thing I forgot to show those people was Swift's name done with a diamond on the window-pane when this place was a school for young chaps,' he said when they had settled in front of the electric heater. 'That would really have interested them.'

'It certainly would have. And it would have greatly interested our literary historian chum.'

'That bounder!' Bobsy brandished the bottle, but Amoelia declined a refill with a wave of her hand. 'The child Swift's name is engraved on the window behind you.'

Amoelia put down her glass and went to the window, screwing up her eyes against the sunlight.

'On one of the lowest panes,' said Bobsy. 'He would have been quite small at the time.'

There was indeed a scrawl on the bottom pane. It read, 'Dean Swift'.

Amoelia couldn't believe what she was seeing. 'How did the child presume he would eventually become a dean?'

'Whatever do you mean?' asked Bobsy.

'His name was Jonathan.'

'I thought it was Dean!' Bobby said.

'People weren't called Dean in those days, it was a purely churchy title, like Archdeacon and Monsignor.'

'Oh,' said Bobsy. He looked somewhat taken aback. 'Well, at least I didn't show it to those people.'

Amoelia chuckled, coughing over her whiskey. 'Lucky for you, or you'd have been the laughing stock of Larne. You thought you were a clever old toad – but not clever enough.'

'And you're far too well educated, you mad cow,' said Bobsy. 'We'll drink to that.'

Christopher Fitz-Simon is a writer and former theatre and television director. He has contributed extensively to BBC radio comedy series as well as adapting and translating the work of existing authors. An honours graduate of Trinity College, Dublin, his doctorate is from the University of Ulster. He has lectured on Irish drama and culture in eleven foreign countries on four continents.